M Harwood

Scattered Flowers

M Harwood

Scattered Flowers

ISBN/EAN: 9783337111151

Printed in Europe, USA, Canada, Australia, Japan

Cover: Foto ©Andreas Hilbeck / pixelio.de

More available books at **www.hansebooks.com**

SCATTERED FLOWERS.

COLLECTED BY

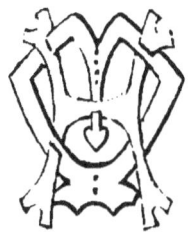

In Memory of

OUR LOST ONE.

LONDON:
Printed by
RICHARD BARRETT, 13, MARK LANE, E.C.

1866.

NOTE.

To the dear friends to whom this little volume is affectionately offered, it may be well to state, by way of apology for many imperfections, that nearly all the contributions were penned when the writers were in their teens.

In Memoriam.

———◦◦◦———

And thou hast left us,—dear one,—ere the sun
   Of nineteen summers shone around thy head :
Thy bright young life,—its story scarce begun,
   Faded before us,—till we mourned thee—dead.
And now, in memory of days gone by,
   And of the path where once thou hoped to shine,
This mingled wreath of love and poesy,—
   Twined with thy own,—we offer at thy shrine ;
Though small its value be—the wish we know was thine.

M. H.

Woodhouse,
   1866.

CONTENTS.

PART FIRST.

THE ROSICRUCIAN.

PART I.

"Oh ! quench my spirit's thirst.
And grant me knowledge ere I die ;
And show life's hidden mystery,
  Or e'er its bubble burst.

" Oh ! grant me endless time,
And the helm in Eternity's meteor boat,
For ever adown Life's stream to float,
  As God ordained in prime.

" Oh ! teach me all mighty lore,
And give me the reins of Life and Death,
And the key of the portal of human breath,
  And the germ of each spirit's core.

" For I fain would walk on the stars of even :
I fain would unbind the cord of life,
And strangle the cry of my spirit's strife.
  That leapeth aloft to Heaven.

L

" Oh ! black is the void behind ;
And black is the fiend-cleft space before,
Where the rolling wheels of the Universe roar
    To the trackless astral wind."

Thus spake a Norseman young,
As he stood on the crater of Hecla's mount,
And gazed adown where the burning fount
    Its pillars of flame up-flung.

'Twas ere the morn arose :—
But the fleeting stars had fled from the West,
Where the flaming incense of Hecla's crest
    O'er the æther's argent glows.

One star alone remained ;
Phosphor, in paling lustre set,—
The last gem of night's coronet,
    When all the rest had waned.

Then the bold and eager knight
Lifted his prayer to the morning star :
From cloud to cloud it fled afar,
    Through the dawning's rosy light.

And soft the answer came,
While a column of gold shot dimly down
In meteor rays, from the scorching crown
    Of the Prince of the Morning Flame.

Across the sky it fled,—
Like a parting smile that gilds the mouth
Of one who, summoned in early youth,
   Is claimed by the hoary dead ;

Or the haze of purple brown,
That flits o'er the dead and the dying leaves,
Ere the icy touch of the winter breeze
   Doth bind them firm adown.

Oh ! soft the answer came—
" I give thee the key of the spirit's strife,
And the clue to the labyrinth of life,
   And the draught of Wisdom's flame.

" But one condition mine,—
Thou shalt not love with thy mortal heart,
Nor rend thy spirit, and yield but part
   At Wisdom's hallowed shrine.

" Thou shalt forswear thy love,—
Nor lean on the breast of mortal maid :
For all things here as a leaf do fade ;
   But thou shalt walk above,

" And dwell with the Son of the Morning Star,
While the countless throngs that round me be,
Shall kneel to thee as they kneel to me,
   When I ride in Eternity's car.

" But first forswear thy bride ;
Give back, give back to the maiden fair
The golden ring and the golden hair,
    That trammel thy spirit's pride."

    The Norseman bowed his head ;
For the spirit of Good within his breast
Drove back the Evil, that, hotly pressed,
    To its chaos of demons fled.

    The Norseman raised his head ;
For the spirit of Evil, ten-fold strong,
Had burst from its adamantine thong, --
    And back to its victim sped.

    Oh ! fiercely the spirits fought :—
The demon of Hell, with its blasphemous sword ;
The angel of Good, with its gentlest word.
    And warning of secret thought.

    But sharp as a cutting wind,
The demon of Evil won the race,—
And tore the last shade of his maiden's face
    From the waverer's fickle mind.

    Then forth from the roaring chasm
Of Hecla's mountain, thunders brake, --
While the voices of fire, like oracles, spake,
    'Mid each volcanic spasm.

With the elemental seal,
His oath was graved as he went his way,
Awaiting sad for the primal ray
    That Wisdom should reveal.

He entered the forest, arched
With the tangled boughs of Odin's trees,
Where no voice spake but the rushing breeze.
    Whose glades no sun e'er parched.

Their "giant boles" up-sprang,—
All gnarled and knotted by surging Time ;
No bird did e'er in their branches chime,
    But fiercely the tempests rang.

The Saga's voice was mute,
And the Norseman's step in this dim arcade,
Was dulled by the groans the hemlock made,
    As it swung on its massive root.

He passed through the stalwart pines,
And came at length to a warrior's tomb,
Where a skeleton glistened through the gloom :
    'Tis the cold Scin Laeca shines.

" Now enter thou child of sin !
And drink of the fountain, boiling up
Through this rifted skull ; 'tis the primal cup
    Ere Wisdom's joys begin."

He drank,—and the fiery vein
Of the magic poison seethed him round ;
And, foaming, he fell to the bloody ground,
   Where a hero's corse had lain.

Then a calm ecstatic joy,
Filled all the void in his raging breast,
Unfurling the banner of lore unblest,
   Enticing him,—to destroy.

He rose upright within the tomb,
Seeming to ride on the buoyant air,
While the cold Scin Lacca, shining there,
   Blue-lighted all the gloom.

And the Son of the Morning Star
Led his soul from height to height ; away
He soared, on the wings of the dawning day,
   In a trance,—afar,—afar.

He learned each deadly bud
That draweth death on its dismal track,
And the passions of every breast doth rack,
   And freeze the circling blood.

And he saw the spirits fair,
And the spirits tall, and mighty, and dread ;
And he called up the souls of the mortal dead,
   And deciphered the speech of the air.

THE ROSICRUCIAN.

He talked with the spirits bold,
Who fled from Elohim's mighty sway,
And dwell deep hid from the eye of day,
   And the reins of darkness hold.

And now he was as God ;—
He knew both good and evil lore,
And the keys of Life's and Death's frail door
   In his darkened breast abode.

And all at the price of—What ?
At the price of all joy and all earthly bliss,
Of maiden's love and of maiden's kiss,
   This Wisdom he had got !

Oh ! drear was his shadowy thought,
As he left the tomb of the warrior dead :
And heard the boughs moan overhead,
   Of the mystery he had bought.

So he passed through the crashing pines,
And back through the forest's tangled way,
Till he came once more where the glowing day
   Down-flashed o'er the snowy lines.

Down-flashed,—but not on him ;
For all was night in his darkened breast,
Where hell's mandragora lay at rest,
   And lulled his conscience dim.

PART II.

MAID ELLA sitteth mournfully ;—
The Norland flowers upon her lap
Are spotless as the snows that wrap
    The hills that fringe the sky.

Maid Ella waiteth musingly ;—
She looketh East, she looketh West,
And starteth up in her unrest :
    A Saga's daughter she.

Oh ! a child of the Northern clime ;
With an angel's form and an angel's face,
And a fleeting step of angel grace,
    O'er the snow and the crystal rime.

But a sadness is in her eye,—
Unmeet for the years when maidenhood
With the glowing woman mingles blood,
    And calms her pulses high.

Maid Ella's eye doth rove
O'er the snowy mountains far away ;
While the red blush on her cheek doth play.
    That tells of an absent love.

The fading buds from her lap she flung,—
" Oh ! why doth he leave me lone,—alone,
So oft by this Saga's hoary stone ?
　My Eric tarries long !

" Not thus was he wont to do,
Till a gloomy fire o'er his spirit came,
And haunted his soul with the mystic flame
　Alluring demons threw.

" I fear, yet I know not why ;
For my Saga mother, dying, said—
' Fear not, fear not—for thy parent dead
　Eternally watches nigh !'

" It is for his soul I fear.
Oh ! Eric, lord of my lonely fate,
Say, why hast thou fled my sight of late ?
　Would, would that thou wert near !

" Where doth the wanderer stay ?
Watch over him mother,—hold him fast.
Lest the fiends may conquer his soul at last,
　And carry him far astray.

" Oh ! Saga mother fair ;
Look down, look down on thy desolate child.
And keep me holy and undefiled,
　Till I fall on thy bosom there, —

" Where the thunders of Odin for ever ring,
And the red wine flows from the skull-cleft bowl,
Keep watch, keep watch o'er my trembling soul.
   Where nature's fountains spring.

" I view thee as thou art ;—
With an oak-crown bound o'er thy shining hair,—
And thine eyes out-flashing into the air
   The fire of thy glorious heart.

" And the light of the samite robe,
That falls and rises o'er thy breast,—
Like a wave of the sea in wild unrest,
   On the trackless ocean globe.

" Oh ! Saga mother dear,
Look down, look down on thy helpless child,
And keep her spotless and undefiled,
   And bring her Eric near."

Scarce were the last words said,
When a faltering step came on anear,
And a faltering voice said, " He is here
   For whom thou hast sadly prayed."

Then joyfully she rose,
And fled to the shelter of his arms ;
Gone for the time her wild alarms,
   Her spirit's darkening woes.

But sadly gleamed his eye,
And coldly he clasped her to his breast ;
For the words of his covenant darkly pressed
    Through the shield of her loving sigh.

" But first forswear thy bride ;
Give back, give back to that maiden fair,
The ring, and the lock of her golden hair.
    That trammel thy spirit's pride."

He knew that he loved her well ;
But the Evil One stilled the voice of his heart,
And he deemed it better with her to part,
    Than with Wisdom's coronal.

" Thou shalt forswear thy love,
Nor clasp to thy breast a mortal maid,
For all things here as a leaf do fade ;
    But thou shalt walk above."

These words in his memory rung,
And drove Love's vision far away,
As he led her back from the gaze of day,
    And himself at her feet down-flung.

" I may not wed with thee,
Cold, cold, alas ! is *my* narrow bed.
And the spirits that wander overhead.
    'Tis not for *thine* eye to see.

"No ; I must dwell alone.
I have forsworn each earthly thought,
And with that oath have dearly bought
   What turns my heart to stone.

" Farewell, sweet child, farewell ;
Shed not one tear o'er my vanished head,
But number Eric with the dead ;
   My Ella dear, farewell."

She comprehended not ;
But lifted her mournful eye to his.
" Alas ! at the price of earthly bliss
   My wisdom I have bought."

She spake,—" What meanest thou,
My Eric ? Sad as the gloomy night.
Thy face seems altered in my sight,
   And darkened all thy brow.

" What means thy faltering speech,
And the look of silent agony
That dwells in the depth of thy shining eye !
   What do these ravings teach ?

" Not wed thee ? If I thought
That came across thy noble mind,
Here, 'neath the blast of the angry wind,
   I'd let my heart's blood out ;

" And fall before thee dead,
As the mass of granite quick down-fell,
That standeth above the raging well,
   Where the Saga's hymns are read.

" Not wed thee ?　Could that be ?
My soul says ' *No*,' from its depth of love,
Whence the wings of my passion rise above,
   And float on the æther free.

" Not wed thee ?　Thou art all
That maketh this cold world dear to me,
And e'er should I languish without thee,
   In Death's cold grasp should fall."

He spake again,—" Alas !
Thou wilt not comprehend my words ;
And must *I* sever thy bosom's cords,
   And let thy soul out-pass ?

" Thou lovest —woe is me !
And I am unworthy of that love ;
Oh ! none but a radiant saint above
   Is worthy thy spirit free.

" Forgive me, oh, forgive !
I have sworn an oath to the powers of Hell,
I have sworn to drink not of Love's well,
   I have sworn alone to live.

"Alas ! I was but man ;
And I longed to grasp the unknown, unseen
But now I am lost to all, I ween,—
    A ROSICRUCIAN !"

    She turned on him in scorn ;
" Go, reprobate degraded wretch !
Though the effort each drop of my life-blood fetch,
    From my breast be thy image torn !

    I would have died for *thee ;*
And thou hast bartered thy soul to Hell,
And left the bride of thy youth as well :
    This—this thou hast done for *me.*

    Back, wretch, to thy lake of fire,
And gloat o'er the power of thy demon charms !
Now, Saga Mother, ope thine arms,
    Receive me,—I expire."

    Oh ! mute she pressed the snows ;
And the dying streak on her paling cheek
Shed o'er their breast a halo meek,
    As upward her spirit goes.

    Then Eric sadly strove
To raise in his arms the lifeless maid ;
But a voice came borne on the winds that said,
" Lo ! all things here as a leaf do fade,
    But thou shalt walk above."

In the eve he dug a grave,
And buried her deep in the lasting snow ;
Snow all around, above, below,
Where no wild breezes rave.

Snow-cold, in her snow-white shroud,
She lay like a statue in snowy rest,
Pure as the snows that wrapped her breast,
In her snow-clad beauty proud.

" Farewell, farewell,"—he said,
Rest on, sweet child, in thine endless sleep,
More fair than the snows that o'er thee weep,
When the rolling storm-clouds downward sweep ;
All here as a leaf doth fade !"

EUSTACE.

1863.

THE URSULINE RECLUSE.

The Convent bell has rung,
  And the sisters kneel in prayer,
While I sink down in my cell alone
  High up by the winding stair.
They say that sleep is sweeter far
  Than the softest perfumes be ;
Yet years have flown since sleep came down
  On its balmy wings to me.

No living voice has greeted me
  For twice five years to-day ;
No human heart has pitied me,
  Tho' grief has turned me grey.
I pray alone,—I dwell alone,
Till Death shall claim me for his own ;
And if that prayer for sin atone,
  Then mine is washed away.

Oh ! days of youth gone by,
  Methinks I am with you *now !*
Ah ! once again I am fair Heléne
  With the clear, smooth marble brow ;
Once more my eyes are bright as stars,
  My smile as the rippling wave ;
Again I rove through the myrtle grove ;
  Again—but hush ! I rave.

My father's castle tower
    Looked down o'er the glittering sea,
And there he built me a fairy bower
    Mid lemon and myrtle tree ;
And hour by hour I sat and dreamed
    Alone on the steep cliff side,
When sunset over the mountains streamed,
And later still, when the moonlight gleamed
    O'er all Sorrento's pride.

The fire-flies glanced around my brow
    As I sat in the moonlight grey :
The pale moths hummed in the orange trees,
And music came on the fragrant breeze,
    Till night seemed turned to day :
And thus in glories like to these
    My girlhood passed away.

There came a knight to our castle tower,
    And a snow-white plume had he ;
Into my bower he threw a flower,
    But what was that to me ?
I could not love this man of gloom,
With the frowning brow, and the snow-white plume :
    For " love dwells with the free !"

My father was a hard, stern man,
    Though he loved me deep and well :
The knight had wealth in distant lands,
    And my father felt its spell.

C

He gave me to the dark-browed knight,
And in the chapel our troth was plight,
While the bell tolled under the taper's light
Telling the hour of the dark midnight—
    Alas! my funeral knell!

Could I have seen in a mystic glass
    The future yet to be,
I had never, never given my hand
To Tancred of the bloody brand—
    Ah! no—thrice woe to me!
Rather than leave my home his bride
I had cast my hopes of heaven aside,
And springing wide from the steep cliff side,
    Had died—in the foaming sea.

But no! the hour of misery
    As yet was far away;
He took my hand in his iron palm
As the boat flew over the waters calm,
    In the dawn of the summer's day.

I could not love this warrior bold,
    For love comes not at will;
And under the shade of the myrtle tree
I had dreamed of a stripling fair to see,
Who sank low down on his bended knee,
And sighed my own sighs back to me,—
    Methinks I hear them still.

And lo ! it came at last,—
   The dream I had dreamed so long :
My soul flew back to the mighty past
On the wings of memory, sweeping fast
Through the pauses of Love's trumpet blast,
   Thro' the notes of the minstrel's song.

He never spake as others oft
   With flattery bold had done ;
But his words were gentle, his voice was soft.
   His smile like the summer sun :
His soul rose upward to his eye,
As often as my form drew nigh ;
How soft and sad the tender sigh
   That echoed back my own !

'Twas night—a glorious night—
   With silvery stars on high ;
The glowing moon, and fire-flies bright,
Flashed downward in a stream of light.
   As Conrad's step drew nigh.
Thou pale, pale moon, pale lower yet -
   Stars, hide your glorious sheen—
Ye fire-flies hear and disappear—
   Amid the myrtles green !

Was our Virgin Queen in Heaven that night
   Looking down from the moonlit zone ?
A power to shield a wandering light !
   A mother to save her own !

They say it thundered loud and far—
I heard it not in my spirit's war—
  For I stood with him—alone !

Sweet mother ! didst thou sleep that night
  And heardest not my prayer,
That veiled in night, my spirit might
  Ascend the golden stair ?
Ascend to thee from out his arms—
  Float upward from his breast—
Where memory eternally,
  Should hold my image pressed ?

A moment, and no more,
  My spirit thought of prayer—
My lips could form no syllable,
I was as one beneath a spell—
  My only God was *there !*

A shadow moved beneath the trees—
  Along the moonlit ground ;
The dark stone-pines waved in the breeze
  Shading the grove around.
Then I heard my husband's stately tread
  I knew the Avenger came,
And I started up in mortal dread
  As he thundered forth my name.

Small space—small need for words—
  The knife was sharper far ;
And deep it sank in Conrad's breast,
  My love, my life, my star !

And Tancred of the bloody brand
Towered over me with crimson hand,
    And dripping scimitar !

" And thou," he cried, " behold,
    And glory in thy power ;
For love of thee two warriors bold
Shall sleep this even pale and cold,
    Their blood shall be the dower
Thy latest lover thou shalt bring ;
    Go lady, and go triumphing !"

Then in the deepening midnight gloom
    He seized the smoking blade,
All crimson with the fearful blow
    On Conrad's breast it made,
And looking upward to the sky
    He plunged it in his own,
Then sighing sadly,—heavily—
    I knew the work was done ;
His corse fell forward at my foot—
The two fond lovers both lay mute—
    And I was left—alone.

Bathed in a molten glory
    Of midnight stars and moon,
They lay there cold before me,
    Crimson their grassy tomb.
Silence, thou rippling river !
    Silence, thou moaning pine !
My day is dark for ever—
    Henceforth the night is mine !

Calm by the rippling river
  Where the pine trees moan,*
Left I them for ever,
  Cold as coldest stone.
Under the ghostly moonshine,
  Under the pine trees roar,
Never to feel the sunshine,
  Never any more !

I wandered all that dreary night
  O'er forest, dale, and hill ;
While mocking me with lambent light
  The stars shone bleak and chill.
I dared not think, I dared not pray,
Lest the demon feet should spurn away
  The soul they could not kill.

I know they mocked my hapless woe
  And laughed in demon glee,
As my thoughts flew up the stairs of Heaven,
  High up—to the jasper sea ;
And I saw a group stand round the Throne,
And each one sighed beneath his crown,
And then they glanced to earth adown,
  And seemed to weep for me !
I know no more—for the gates of Heaven
Clanged loudly over the unforgiven ;
And here I dwell alone, unshriven,
  Till Death shall set me free !

Naples, 1864.   EUSTACE.

---

* Where the long reeds quiver,
    Where the pines make moan , &c.—MRS. HEMANS.

NARCISSUS.

SUGGESTED BY A STATUE IN THE VATICAN.

THE winds are rushing sadly through the pines
And olives, through the oak and through the thorn ;
The moon in silver silence lights the stream,
And slumbers in its depth of hazy gloom.
Her argent glory, flickering o'er my brow
And bosom, sends a chill through all this frame
That lies reflected in the gleaming pool
For ever—clear and calm for evermore.

I gaze down sadly from the daffodils
And dark green rushes at my image, there
For ever mirrored both by day and night,--
In light and darkness,—twilight hour or dawn,—
Noonday or midnight.

         Ever, ever there,
A fair round form before me sleeps and sleeps
In glittering silence.   'Tis mine own—mine own !
The roses cast no bloom upon the cheeks,
The daffodils shine not around the brow,
Nor doth the lotus light those liquid eyes,
Nor any living hue suffuse the flesh
That bloomed so roseate once.   My image lies
Calm as a statue, white as marble, cold
As frozen snow, within the river's gloom,
Where no voice ever comes—no human voice,
Nor eye, nor hand, save mine.

Here cold I gaze,
Chained by my own mad folly,—lone, fast-bound
To mine own image in the glassy mere.
Cursèd for ever be that even-tide,
When, fleeing Echo's voice, I crouched amidst
The daffodils beside the star-lit stream :
And, seeing mine own likeness in the wave,
Stood gazing silently, and dared not move,
So glorious seemed the shadow of this form.

And thus I stand and gaze for evermore ;
The solemn silence round me passes not
Away,—but seems to grow in depth and length
Of stillness, as the seasons come and go.
No sound breaks in upon the eternal peace,
No ripple shakes the river's sullen gloom,
No voice of bird makes glad the air around,
No bee hums o'er the lilies.   All is still
And lone, and sad as death, and still I gaze !

Mine own eye never moves, but motionless
Pierces the water, traverses the depth
Of hazy sapphire where my image lies,
Fast bound by chains invisible ; my hand
Stirs not to scare away the butterfly,
Whose golden crimson rests upon my brow
In floods of sunshine ; nor to wring the dew
That gathers coldly in my flowing hair
At midnight, nor to shield my burning brain
From blaze of lightning, or from glare of sun.

The beast within the forest dies ; the bird
Upon the mountain ; fish within the sea,
All things alive, in field, or flood, or fell,
Return to earth rejoicing.   Why not I ?
Alas ! here motionless, enchained by pride,
Enduring silence—solemn agony
Of never-ending stillness—cold and drear.
For ever gazing on that beauty, prized
So highly once,—now loathsome to mine eye,
And heart, and soul.   I, Narcisse, meet my doom,
Lapped in the daffodils, yet sharing not
The sweet nepenthe of the Elysian fields,
That wafts the immortal to the land of dreams,
And hushes Heaven to sleep.

                    If I could mar
The form imperial that the Gods bestowed,
And rend these limbs apart, or tear the flesh
From off the quivering muscles, or deface
This countenance that once I deemed so fair,—
Gladly I'd throw this beauty to the winds,
And thus redeem my crown of amaranth,
My starry sceptre and Elysian dreams ;
And, falling in the arms of Mother Earth,
Among the blooming lilies sink to sleep,—
Still silence round me but for Echo's voice,
All mournful, singing dirges evermore.

                                        EUSTACE.

Rome, 1864.

THE DEATH-DREAM OF MARY HAMILTON.

THE end is near.   I hear the echoing fall
  Of angel footsteps round me as I lie,
Drear in the hours between the vesper call
  And midnight.   Ah, how oft I prayed to die,
Not knowing Him whose love is all in all.

Yet am I ready.   Bear me from my cell—
  And lay me down beneath the shadowy trees—
Still within hearing of the chiming bell ;
  For I would feel once more the passing breeze,
And hear the tale the quivering aspens tell.

I weary of the dark conventual gloom
  Of sacred shrine and imaged saint on high,
And colours streaming down o'er marble tomb,
  Thro' crimson casement whose rich tintings vie
In crowning martyrs—fresh from awful doom.

Carry me down beside the winding stream
  Where once a sudden glory wrapped me round,
And mute I listened in a rapturous dream
  To words that left me there, a maid—spell-bound,
Unwitting then how fair the false can seem.

But oh ! *he* was not false ; his soul was high,
   And full of lofty aspirations.   None
Dare thus accuse him ; how much less, then, I
   Who owned him lord and life, and star and sun.
And deemed I talked with God when he was nigh.

They buried him at dawning bleak and cold,
   Laid him to sleep beneath the mountain pine ;
The soft snow wrapped him in its ' ermine fold,'
   The eagle shrieked his death dirge,—ah, and *mine* ;
The clouds of destiny o'er both had rolled.

I watched and waited all that dreary night
   Alone and speechless,- racked by grief and woe ;
While pacing on and on, through heaven so bright,
   The silver moon all silently did go.
But I paced up and down the mountain's height ;

And stood afar, when rosy shadows spread
   Above a funeral cortège drawing nigh ;
Then to the dust I bowed my aching head,
   And prayed—how wildly— that I too might lie
Cold in the shadow of the silent dead.

That prayer is granted.   Ere the midnight star
   Hath climbed the silver firmament, my soul
Shall seek admission at the crystal bar ;
   And while the clouds of glory round me roll,
My opening eyes shall know what angels are.

Then carry me once more beneath the trees
  Where the rank grasses tall and wildly wave,
And murmuring gales play gently with them there,
  Above the fated poet's nameless grave.
I fain would view that grave, and feel that breeze,—

And meet my doom where he lies pale and cold ;
  So that the angel, when his trumpet sound,
May find us both together, and unfold
  His banner over us ; so all around
May know that woman's love can ne'er grow old.

The clouds depart,—my soul is lighter,—lo !
  A shadowy glory falls athwart the wave,
Where diamonds ripple onward,—sad and slow,—
  Around the grass that shades the poet's grave.
The sun is sinking.   Thus earth's visions go,

And come before me mirrored as in glass ;
  The tournament—the feast—the regal throne—
The thundering music—and the glittering mass
  Of nobles round.   Ah me ! all—all is done !
Love, hope, joy, sorrow—all with life outpass,

Unmourned—unmourning.   Hark ! the solemn prayer
  Invites my longing spirit to depart
From all earth's fantasies, and meet *him*—there,
  Where none shall pass between me and his heart.
The silver moonlight steals adown the stair,

Through gorgeous casements where rich colours tell
    Of saint and martyr.   There doth Mary stand—
The child-Christ on her bosom ;—there as well,
    The crownèd seraphs, and the flaming brand
Waves in the air,—the Archangel Raphael.

Farewell, soft moonshine.   Never—never more—
    (Unless on silent effigy of stone)
Shalt thou above my shadowy tresses pour,
    Or charm my spirit—praying here—alone :
Crowning my brow with light, and passing o'er.

Fainter and fainter grows the echoing hymn,
    And I die with it.   Further—further still.
Its notes recede—till up in heaven they seem
    Lost mid the thousand harps on Sion's hill.—-
My God, I come !   Thus ends my earthly dream.

                                        EUSTACE.

ÆOLIAN.

My soul is troubled—it may not rest,
Ever I roam by grief opprest,
White is the shroud that wraps my breast,
Yet in the grave I find no rest.
I wander on—for ever on—
Death-cold, pale and woe-begone.
Other forms may softly rest,
But in the grave for me is none.
                    Æolian ! Æolian !

Born of the old Etruscan race,
Regal blood was in my form,
Regal beauty in my face,
Regal vengeance in my arm.
Now, wild beasts alone should gaze
On my white, sin-stricken face ;
Never shall I find a place
Within the fair celestial space.
                    Æolian ! Æolian !

Had I known what now I know,
What it is from life to go,
And from glorious earth to be
Hurled into Eternity ;
Had I gazed behind the veil,
I had trembled and turned pale,
And escaped the serpent's trail,
Everlasting woe and wail.
                    Æolian ! Æolian !

Æolian ! Æolian !
How fair the name—how false the man !
I loved him only as daughters can
Of the ancient race Etrurian.
Woe to him, and woe to me !
Woe to our earth-freed spirits be !
Let him sigh through Eternity,
For the years of sighing he brought to me.
                    Æolian ! Æolian !

I sat beneath an orange tree,
    Building castles in the air ;
The yellow fruit hung over me,
    And the yellow branches fanned my hair :
Odours of myrtle faint yet deep,
Hushed my soul to a gentle sleep ;
I watched the flowers and the timid sheep,
And a knight who climbed the hill-side steep :
                    Æolian ! Æolian !

And at my side a warrior knelt,
His fiery gaze was all I felt ;
His raven locks half touched my cheek ;
I sat spell-bound, I could not speak.
Flaming eyes and cheeks of flame,
    Kisses of fire that scorched my brow ;
Wild he called upon my name,
    With fondest oath and wildest vow,
                    Æolian ! Æolian !

The day seemed darker as he went,
    The very sun shone cold and dim ;
The perfume of the flowers was spent,
    And daylight fled away with him !
The moon rose up, bright, round, and full,
But seemed no longer beautiful.
The golden stars, so high, so fair,
Shone baleful in the fleecy air.
                    Æolian ! Æolian !

The warrior never came again,
False tongue, false heart, and falser man ;
And on my soul was an endless stain,
                    Æolian ! Æolian !
But never more with eye of flame
And burning kiss the warrior came ;
Though evermore I wept the same,
And ever thought " My shame, my shame !"
                    Æolian ! Æolian !

Shrieking, moaning, all the night,
Moaning, shrieking, all the morn,
I watched alone on the mountain's height
Lying there—forlorn—forlorn !
Watching, waiting, early, late,—
I proved his falsehood day by day ;
I struggled not against my fate,
But my good angel fled away.
                    Æolian ! Æolian !

I hunted him, as a lioness
  Hunts her weak and timid prey ;
On and on in my distress,
  I followed him for leagues away.
My weary footfall heavily
  Trod down the sunbeams in the grass,
My weary soul sighed fervently,
  Watching each moon-lit evening pass.
              Æolian ! Æolian !

And when the sunset streamed on high,
  O'er rippling wave and lonely fell,
There rose up mocking to the sky
  The clear sad voice of convent bell.
" Child of Earth," it seemed to say,
" All things here shall pass away—
  Earth and Heaven, wind and wave ;—
In the twinkling of an eye
Time becomes Eternity ;
  Here no rest but in the grave."
              Æolian ! Æolian !

To Heaven my tearless eyes I turned,
When red star-watchfires dimly burned,
And seemed to mock my agony ;
Oh ! that I like them could be !
Cold and bleak and hard as stone ;
They *are* hard, they never moan,
When all earth-born children groan ;
In the high heavens they sit alone,
Each on his pinnacled flaming throne.
              Æolian ! Æolian !

I traced the false one on and on,
    Day by day I drew more near,
At last the victory was won,
    And a voice said, " Behold him here !"
I found him in Ferrara's walls,
    And then my heart stood still with woe,
For another dwelt in his " marble halls,"
    A lady, fair as fairest snow.
                            Æolian ! Æolian !

False ! false !   Traitor pale,
Cower before my spirit's wail.
Let this heart which broke for thee,
Witness my soul's agony.
All that day I waited lone,
    Dared not think, and dared not pray ;
Cold my hand as the mountain stone—
    Dire my thought as the wild sea spray.
                            Æolian ! Æolian !

Dagger in hand, and hate in heart,—
    Armed with vengeance dark and deep—
I fled along with Azrael's dart,
    When all the town was hushed in sleep ;
I passed by many a stately door,—
    Fled, and looked not back again ;
The Angel of Death was passing o'er,—
    But one alone he summoned then ;
                            Æolian ! Æolian !

On through stately corridor,—
Over mosaic and marble floor ;
Past the statues gleaming hoar,
As a flood of moonlight washed them o'er.—
On I fled to a silent room
Where the misty moonbeam lit the gloom,
And the cold white stars kept watch on high,
Growing red as my steps drew nigh :
                    Æolian ! Æolian !

I kissed him softly in his sleep,—
    Lapped in dreamland far away ;
Moonbeams through the casement peep
    That soon shall rest on his pallid clay.
Heaving breast and quiet eyes !
    Sleeping smile and marble brow !
Never more shall that warrior rise,—
    Earth and Heaven had heard my vow.
                    Æolian ! Æolian !

Life is ending, death beginning,
    Human soul that sleepest on,
In the last race, Death is winning,
    Life is weeping—overthrown.
Proud one, Death is at thy gate,
    Take the crown from off thy brow :
Would'st thou live ? Too late ! Too late '
    At thy threshold waits he now.
                    Æolian ! Æolian !

Awake ! but on this earth— no more ;
   Awaken at the trumpet's sound,
When thou shalt land on another shore ;—
   Till then—sleep on in the humid ground.
Sleep— as sleep the sinners—cold,
With piles of turf above thee rolled,
And glories that thou canst not hold,
Passing above thee, manifold.
           Sleep on—sleep on, Æolian.

He lay before me—dead at last—
   Great white limbs as marble cold,
Crimson streams from his bosom passed
   Over his garments' silken fold.
Still white limbs, and proud white face,
   These were all that met my gaze ;
But I fled like fire from the awful place,
   Away—far out in the starry space,
           While he slept on—Æolian !

They tied me to the burning stake,
   Angry flames leaped up on high,
Swathed me round in molten lake,
   And *then* I knew what 'twas to die !
Yet from my lips escaped no moan,
   Though I knew that life at last was done ;
While low in his home 'neath shade and sun,
   The warrior-prince slept on and on ;
         Æolian ! Æolian !

And in that awful dying hour,
    When thousands gathered round to see,—
I felt within, the solemn power
    To read Creation's mystery ;
And nearer to the unveiled truth
    In that last hour of life discrowned ;
I scanned the shades of life and death,
    The human mystery profound ;
                Æolian ! Æolian !

And shadowed forth as in a glass
I saw the rolling ages pass,
And kingly crown and diadem
Were lost to earth, and earth to them.
And time fled on —immortal sea,
That falls into Eternity ;—
And wrecked were days, and months and years,
And human hopes and human fears ;
But in my breast one voice spake on,
                Æolian ! Æolian !

                        EUSTACE.

Woodhouse, 1863.

THE DESERTED GROVE.

(Villa d'Este.)

Calm, in an orange grove, lit up by the quivering moonbeam,
Stand in a circle of flowers, twelve mystic statues
colossal.
There like the gods of Olympus, calm and erect and
majestic,
Clear-cut in marble, and chiselled, and sculptured, in
might and in grandeur ;
Gazing adown on the scene immovable—rigid—regard-
less—
Calm in their marble repose—majestic and cold in their
silence.

Ever they sleep—snow-white—stiff—moulded in mani-
fold grandeur.
There frowns Jove ; and Apollo clasps lightly the lyre
on his bosom ;
High o'er the wave of the sea, her white arm lifts
Aphrodite,
Shrieking and shrieking in vain, "Ai! Ai!" to the
glorious billows ;—
There Saturnius and Juno keep vigils in marble, des-
pairing ;

Bacchus, and Pallas, and Mars, and Hermes, and Pluto,
    and Vesta,
Gazing adown cold, cold ; and Ceres the number com-
    pleteth.

Ever they sleep, snow-white, festooned by the glittering
    flowerets ;
Roses, and jasmine, and myrtle kiss softly the limbs of
    the heroes,
Shaded on high by the crimson convolvulus, lily, and
    dew-bell,
Casting a flush o'er the rounded limbs and the colourless
    faces,
Either in sunshine or moonshine ; and oranges falling
    around them ;—
Weirdly the oleander supporteth these giants of marble
Bright with its scarlet twining ; and so they grow old in
    their silence.

EUSTACE.

Rome, 1864.

ANTINÖUS.

(A DREAM OF HADRIAN'S VILLA.)

THE azure heavens were purpling into night,
With crimson glories flashing up the sky,
And falling lurid o'er the still blank wave,
Where all were gazing.   Calm the river lay,
Hushed into silence lest its voice should wake
The soft sleep of the lilies : in its depth,
Mirrored in silver, shone the evening star.

But over all the scene was thrown a cloud
Of doubt and consternation ; for they saw
Shining among the quivering scarlet blooms
A form—a human form ; then staring eyes
Looked forth on blanching cheeks, and many a heart
Stood still with trembling fear.

                              " How came it there ?"
" Whose form, whose features ?"   " Nay, perchance he
        sleeps."
" This is not Death,—the rounded limbs are white
And almost warm ; the rose is not yet fled
From off that downy cheek."   " The lips, the eye

Are scarce less life-like, and the sunbeam falls
As ever on the midnight of his hair."
" He will awake."   " He sleeps, he surely sleeps."
" So soundly—ah, so soundly !"

                              Then they drew
The fair, white human form from out the wave,
Across the blossoms to the nearest bank ;
And ere they had laid it on the soft green earth
Beneath the palm trees, every voice brake forth
In one loud wailing—" Ah ! Antinöe !"

One crimson ray fell o'er him from the West,
As flickering in its radiance sank the sun
Behind the palm trees ; in the stagnant wave
Arose a murmur as of strife below,
That earth should steal its prey.—Alas ! alas !
Earth—Mother Earth—but claimed the human clay.
The soul was drifting through those crimson clouds,
Or falling down the darkness ; or, perchance,
Was motionless, as if it ne'er had been.

The priests of Isis came and wrapped him round
With rites mysterious, but he heard them not.
Pale Nubian maidens, lotus-crowned and tall,
With scared black irids came and looked at him
In silent awe,—while others wrung their hands,
Rose-steeped in attar, o'er the unconscious form,
And cried out in one voice of bitter wail,
" Antinöe !" till all the desert rang
With that one mournful name, while Egypt wept.

Then flashing down the river, swiftly came
A gorgeous pageant at that solemn sound,—
'Twas Hadrian's galley. There the Emperor sat
But missed his Nubian favourite from his side,
And wondered. Clothed in scarlet were they all,
With jewels on their robes, and flowery crowns
Around their long bright perfumed locks ; the light
From out the West blazing o'er gold and gem,
Till all the galley seemed a mass of flame
And glory.

   But Antinöus ! Where was he ?
Warriors were sighing, women shedding tears,
Priests muttering, maidens wailing, o'er him now.
Imperial Hadrian caught that bitter wail,—
And as the trumpet's war-note strikes a chill
To many a heart of mother,—ay, and wife,—
So on the Emperor's soul that message fell.
And leaping to the stream, he climbed the bank,
And fled along in maddening rage and fear,
To that far group, where terror-stricken maids,
And priests and warriors stood. One glance told all,
As each made way in wonderment, and gazed
After the faltering monarch as he ran.

Then falling o'er the youth he wept aloud,
And cursed the river,—ay, and cursed the gods,—
And all things human and divine ; and laid
His hand upon the Nubian's heart,—and called
And wept again ; but never answer came.

Then laid they him to sleep in gorgeous pomp,
With clash of arms amid the city's roar,
Beneath a gilded roof, be-gemmed and girt
With dazzling ornament ; upon his brow
A crown of scarlet lilies ; round his form
Imperial robes of light with belt of gold,
And armlets all ablaze with jewelled gleam ;
And on his finger Hadrian's signet ring.

Sadly the monarch took him in his arms,
And laid him in the tomb,—while all stood round
In mournful phalanx ; then they threw far down
Upon him lotus blooms and amaranth ;
And softly closed the four walls of his home;
While underneath the banners Hadrian stood ;
And clear and calm the Imperial dreamer's voice
Went up through silence to the winds of Heaven.

And Hadrian said,—" He sleeps not as they sleep
Who pass their years in idleness, and strife,
And folly ; he shall wake—shall live again ;
And I shall see him, *where* I know not,—*how*
I guess not,—*why* I dare not think,—nor *when*.
But this I know,—that something from that clay
Has parted,—that now shines far off and dim,
Yet ever growing brighter and more bright ;
In grades of glory, as that silver star
Grew brighter in the stagnant river-gloom ;
And that same light I shall hereafter meet
In other skies, when I too shall have gone
Beyond the sunset.   We shall meet again !

EUSTACE.

Rome, 1864.

THE FROZEN SENTINEL.

(Suggested by an occurrence which took place at Rome in the Winter of 1863.)

At the midnight hour pale moonbeams pour
O'er the ancient hall of the Senator,
   And its fountain's frozen sea ;
And crystals hoar shine on the door,
Then splash down softly on the floor
   Where the frozen snow-flakes be.

Up and down, and on and on,
The sentinel paces 'neath the moon
   And stars of the Roman sky.
" My weary vigil will end full soon."
He sits him down on an antique stone,
   And looks at the stars on high.

Is it a dream that holds him there
With eyes enchained to the upper air,
   Where nought but the pale stars be ?
His head sinks down in his frozen hand,
Perchance he thinks of his fatherland,
While the statues grand in the moonlight stand.
   Around the fountain's sea.

And now he thinks on his distant home,
While the shades of dreamland round him come.
He hears anon the rolling drum
    That called him thence away ;
And now he starts at the moaning breeze
That flits through his native forest trees,
And now he sees, on her bended knees,
    His well-loved mother pray.

His calm white face on his breast sinks down,
No more he heeds the statues' frown ;—
Slumber is on him,—sleep is upon him,
    Under the shade of the pillars brown ;
A stalwart column stands o'er him, solemn,
    Stern, unbending as the will,
Now forcing sleep to his eyes to creep,
Slumber lasting—strong and deep—
    That must its victim kill.

One more dream to his fancy flies—
A fairy vision of laughing eyes,
    And sunny golden hair ;
Cheeks that blushed when his voice was hushed,
And the hours of another midnight rushed,
    Swift-footed through the air.

This, oh this is a dream of bliss,—
Sad was the maiden's farewell kiss,
    And the tear in her bright blue eye.
But a colder kiss doth greet him *now*,
The midnight snow falls on his brow,
    As the Angel of death draws nigh.

Snnk on his breast his head doth rest,
Dreaming the dream he loves the best.
    Watching him, solemn,
    The stalwart column
Holds him fast to its granite breast.

And lo ! through the path of the moon-lit gloom,
Over the snow does Azrael come,
To call the sentinel's spirit home ;
    "Away ! Away ! Away !"
And the ghastly moonshine wraps a shroud
Around the form of the soldier proud,
And the wind moans loud o'er his visage bowed,
Sweeping the pall of a dark storm-cloud
Above his frozen clay.

There in his place, with proud, calm face,
They found the sentinel, when the rays
    Of the sun fell o'er the snow ;
But still and cold, as the statues old
Of furious steeds, and riders bold,
That guard the halls of the Capitol,
    Was the heart that lay below.

                                        EUSTACE.

Rome, 1864.

THE CREATION OF MAN.

*(Suggested by Michael Angelo's fresco on the roof of
the Sistine Chapel at Rome.)*

THE earth lay wrapped in folds of pearly mist,
And shrouded with the purple hues of even,
Vast in its equipoise,—a rolling sphere.
And silence reigned throughout the universe
Of starry systems opening one by one
From out the radiance of illumined skies,
That guard with solemn light Jehovah's Throne.

But lo ! a gorgeous vision bathes the West,
Wrapped in the splendours of the setting sun,
And crowned with awful glory ;—half in light
Shines forth,—and half lies hid in crimson shade,
Whence mellowing off in robes of azure hue,
The floating pinions rise, and fall and rise,
Beneath the veil that shrouds the Almighty Form.

And hovering downward o'er the verdant earth,
Still,—silent as the æther up on high,
The Lord cast off his veil and smote the ground ;
Then from the dust arose a shape of light,
Fair—glorious—perfect—the true image of
The Eternal Father,—and He called it *Man*.

Fair limbs from out the dust he fashioned,
Clothing them with celestial flesh and blood,
And joints and sinews each in right degree,
And form and features glorious as his own.

And when the work was finished, then He breathed
The breath of Life within the noble frame.
And slow receding through the purple clouds,
Veiled in a crimson shadow,—drew his hand
O'er all the form in benediction calm,
From head to foot,—till lingeringly He touched
The last white finger,—and so passed away.

                                        ، EUSTACE.

Rome, 1864.

THE TWO QUEENS.

THE death-chant is singing—the joy-bells are ringing,—
   The one for a victim,—the other a queen :
Jane Seymour impatient awaits coronation,—
   And low in a dungeon lies—Anna Boleyn.

The one rises lightly, and gaily and brightly,
   And draws out the pearls through the waves of her
      hair ;
The other wild presses her hand to her tresses,
   And feels for a crown that, alas ! is not there.

One views in the distance a rosy existence,
   Where sunshine shall flicker, and flow'rs ever grow :
The other cries scornfully, calmly, yet mournfully—
   " Vanity—vanity all things below !"

The joy-bells are ringing—the death-chant is singing—
   Come forth to the altar ! Come forth to the tomb !
The Bridegroom is laughing—the headsman is quaffing :
   The Bride waits her triumph—the Victim her doom.

                          E

The death-chant is singing—the joy-bells are ringing ;
  The one o'er a corse, and the other—a bride ;
The one queen is sleeping,—the other is keeping
    Bright watch with the bridegroom who kneels at her
      side.

But high up in Heaven, where sin is forgiven,
  The souls of the martyrs claim Anna Boleyn :
And flowers ever vernal, and glories eternal
  Surround the white soul of the sanctified queen.

EUSTACE.

THE MARRIAGE OF THE SEA.

(A LEGEND OF ADRIA.)

THE Doge he leant him o'er the prow,
 And a scornful laugh laughed he ;
" Receive, receive thy marriage ring,
 Thou opal Adrian Sea !"

The barge was decked with gold and white,
 And sailed beneath the sun ;
Warriors brave and ladies bright
 Upon its deck sat down.

Oh ! bursts of echoing music came
 O'er the waters rolling far,
As the barge sped on like the sun's red flame
 When it kindles the evening star.

And peals of mocking laughter flew
 From the breasts of that companie ;
One maid alone sat woe-begone
 At the Marriage of the Sea.

E 2

She gazed at the Doge right earnestly,
  Then sadly turned aside,
And the wavelets drank up eagerly
  The tears she strove to hide.

"'Twas with that ring he pledged his love
  And plighted troth to me ;
In vain with my raging breast I strove,—
  I vowed his love to be.

" I loved him deep—I loved him long,
  With a maiden's mighty will ;
I loved him wild—I loved him strong,
  And oh ! I love him still !

" I gave to him that sapphire ring
  When he gave his love to me,—
To me no more his heart 'twill bring,
  It lies in the deep blue sea.

" When first I laid it in his hand,
  He low at my feet knelt down ;
Now the roaring brine will sweep its sand
  Around that sapphire stone.

" Alas ! 'twill shine on his hand no more
  Where erst it lustre gave ;
A priceless gem on a golden shore
  'Twill lie neath a sapphire wave.

" But not for that doth my spirit grieve ;
    'Tis not for that—ah, no !
I mourn that his love so brief should live—
    I mourn for my endless woe.

" Ye men, your hearts are as adamant
    When your fleeting love is gone.
Nought rests for me save the restless sea,
    Or the convent's cloister lone."

She turned her face to the azure sky,
    And checked her tears the while ;
Till the mellowing light that flamed on high.
    Drew o'er her face a smile.

So heavenly seemed her beauteous face,
    The Doge looked up in awe ;
And the youths each rose from out his place,
    As if a saint he saw.

Then spake the Doge—" Sweet Leonore,
    What see'st thou in the sun,
That thy irids bright inhale his light,
    Yet cast their glance on none ?"

" I see the mirror of truthful love,"
    In a low voice answered she ;
" I see the reflex carved above
    Of the love I bear to thee.

" I see portrayed on his shining flame,
　　On his flashing golden zone,
The form that first to my spirit came
　　Ere my deep love had begun."

She turned her face to the opal sea
　　With a look of frenzy wild,—
The waves below rolled gloriously,
　　As the sunlight o'er them smiled.

Her face grew strong and pale and cold,
　　As she gazed the deeps adown,—
And the maidens in terror started up
　　From beneath their flowery crown.

" What seest thou there, sweet Leonore ?"
　　Said the Doge, in a solemn tone:
" Why turns thy face so pallid o'er,
　　And rigid as statue-stone ?"

" I see in the deep sea more,—far more
　　Than I saw in the blazing sun ;
But never its depth will the ring restore
　　Thy bridegroom's hand hath thrown.

" I see it lie—oh ! fathoms deep—
　　Whence none may the gem up-bring ;
And the glancing fishes round it creep,
　　Like guards round a sacred thing.

" I mourn,—but not that the sun above
    Shall ne'er shine on its beauteous dyes ;—
I mourn for the death of the mighty love
    That with it buried lies.

" Thou hast laid it deep with the symbol ring—
    Far down in a roaring gloom ;
Nought, nought can that buried love up-bring,
    And mine—is its fathomless tomb."

She sprang to the breast of the rolling wave
    Like a lily to the blast,—
And ere they could stretch an arm to save.
    Beneath her form had passed.

And down she sank,—they saw her clear,—
    Far down through the wavelets fair ;
Till calm, the mystic ring so near,
    She rested—safely there.

Then rose to the surface, sweeping up
    Like a mermaid bathed in foam ;
And the symbol ring did the maiden bring,
    Safe—safe from its watery home.

" Hail ! hail to the nymph of Adria,
    Who thus can breast the wave :
'Tis the fairest diver of the land !
    The bravest of the brave !

" Hail to the fairest maiden !   Hail
  To the Queen of the Adrian Sea !"
Thus spake the Doge to the damsel pale,
  As he sank on his bended knee ;

And clasped her wild to his beating heart,
  And prayed her to forgive ;
Then soft vowed he, on his bended knee,
  For her alone to live.

She smiled around right joyously,
  On the sun and the wave smiled she ;
" Behold, I up-bring thy marriage ring !
  Thou'rt still a maid, oh Sea !"

She cast it down, right merrily down,
  And laughed out long and free :
" Flow bright, flow soft, flow calm around,
  Thou'rt wedded *now*, oh Sea !"

EUSTACE.

IRENE.

(A LEGEND OF THE VILLA LANTE.)

WE laid her slowly—softly down,
  Beside the star-lit sepulchre,
  Where all the saints might look at her ;
And then—they left me there alone.
The stars gazed downward solemnly
  O'er sculptured arch, and moon-lit stair.
  Thro' crimson casements past compare,
Where sainted forms shone gloomily.
The roses on her brow I laid,—
  The fair white lilies in her hand,—
  Upon her breast the mystic band
Of amaranth, that ne'er shall fade.
Two snow-white roses from her brow
  I took,—and kissed them solemnly,
  In sign of vengeance yet to be ;
And see ! their hue is blood-red now.
The others at her feet I laid.
  A crucifix upon her breast,—
  To guard her in her dreamless rest—
Then for her soul's repose I prayed !

EUSTACE.

Rome, 1864.

THE PEARL FISHER.

*(Suggested by a Statue from the Studio of Paul Akers
at Rome.)*

BENEATH the shining waters of the gorgeous Indian sea,
There lieth many a treasure line of shipwrecked argosy ;
And many a sunny island springs glittering from the
     main,
Where sleeps the young pearl fisher, never to wake
     again.

The weeds are twining softly in and out his golden hair,
And leafy sprays of crimson shine around his body fair,
And very silently he lies within his boundless grave,
Oh ! very calm, and safe at rest beneath the sapphire
     wave.

The winds of Heaven play softly o'er the gorgeous
     Indian sea,
Whose deep blue waters lap him round, asleep, where
     no winds be ;
The coral islands start up into life, and close him round
With walls of scarlet adamant, and solitude profound.

The very pearls around him that in life he held so dear,
Lie patiently beside his hand,—he knows not they are
     near ;

The glancing fishes dart aside in wonderment and fear.
The sea is deep,—the sea is wide,—his grave is bright
    and clear.

Fast in the scarlet meshes of the cruel weed he lies,—
Coldly the sunlight flashes down across his closèd eyes ;
Bright is his couch with purple in a gorgeous reedy
    gloom,
Where silent coral insects build the four walls of his
    tomb.

Of scarlet is the vaulted roof,—scarlet the glowing wall,
And in the midst his body lies in a dazzling scarlet
    pall,—
Glittering white in all the glory of his beauty proud ;
On his arm his head is pillowed,—over the sea-shells
    bowed.

Calm in the sea-girt silence where no ripple dares to
    moan,
He sleeps among the islands, very softly—all alone.
Can the bright angels see him—fathom-deep down in
    the sea !
Can they penetrate the darkness of the ocean's mystery ?

The God who made can see him,—fathom-deep down
    where he lies,—
With the water sealing up his ear, and closing fast his
    eyes ;

And when the sea shall cast its dead upon the Heavenly
    shore,
The fisher shall awake and hear, and live for evermore.

Then Christ shall lay his finger on the fast-closed ear
    and eye,
And bear him from the sapphire sea, up through the
    sapphire sky.
Till then the brave pearl fisher sleepeth brightly, calmly
    on—
In his rest beneath the Indian sea, where none shall
    wake him, *none !*

EUSTACE.

Rome, 1864.

DIRGE.

" WHERE the moon and stars
Float up softly through the azure sky ;
Where the stones gleam white in the moonbeam,
And the willows weep in the sunbeam,
Let me lie !

Where the thrush and the lark
Fling their voices to the gates of Heaven ;
Where the nightingale
Tells its merry tale
When the sunset gilds the sky at even,—
Let me lie !"

" Where the restless wave
Sings the requiem of the brave and fair :
Where the billows only
Break the silence lonely,
And the sighing murmur
Of the wind that thunders round the hero's grave.
And o'er thy tomb so rare ;
Among the coral islands,
Thou shalt sleep for days, and months, and years !

And the silence
Shall not pass away,—
But day by day,
Grow more deep and lasting ;
Waves shall seal thine ear,
Sleeping,—waking,—dreaming,—by the islands
That the coral worms are casting
For thy bier !"

                              EUSTACE.

PART SECOND.

LINES

ADDRESSED TO AN INFANT, WHO LISTENED WITH DELIGHT
TO THE STRAINS OF A MUSICAL BOX.*

Oh ! surely that earnest and thoughtful brow
   Belongs not, fair child, to thee ;
And why is the laugh that I heard but now
   Checked in its gushing glee ?
What " change" has passed o'er thy "spirit's dream."
   E'en yet in its infancy ?
What shadow hath quenched the sunny beam
   Of thy bright and joyous eye ?

I marvel not,—for the magic power
   That is borne on Music's wing,
Is pressing upon thy frame this hour.
   Too much for so frail a thing.
Oh ! fain would'st thou soar from earth away.
   Its fetters are hard to bear,
While visions so beautiful round thee play.
   Whose glories thou canst not share.

Thou art dreaming, perchance, of a sunny world.
   Wherein thy lot is cast,—
Where the banner of gladness is ever unfurled,
   And unknown is the tempest's blast ;

* The infant alluded to was Eustace Harwood.

Where the balmy breezes are always mild,—
  Bright skies, and thornless flowers ;
Oh ! would for thy sake, and our own, sweet child,
  That such were this world of ours !

But sorrow and sadness have entrance here,
  And bitter is discord's breath,—
While the spirit of darkness ever is near
  To lure us to sin and death !
One flower alone is without a thorn,
  May'st thou prize it all else above,—
From thy breast may it never be rudely torn,—
  'Tis the " thornless rose of love ! "

Its presence will lessen life's bitterest draught,
  Though full that cup may be,—
While the sweetest that mortal e'er has quaffed
  Is mingled, by Love, for thee !
Then cherish its growth in thy youthful heart,
  It will bless thy fostering care,—
And, by bidding all discord and strife depart,
  Will create an Eden there.

Hast thou visions too of a far-off land,
  Whose streets are paved with gold ?
Where beings in white walk hand in hand,
  And glittering harps they hold.
Oh ! tales of glory to infant ear,
  In such tones may well be given,—
They speak in the voice of their own bright sphere ;
  For Music's home is Heaven.

And all thy dreams of that blessed place
  Too glorious cannot be,
For the visions of earth never yet kept pace
  With the fair reality !
Even these sweet echoes floating by,
  Cannot lift thy fancy dim
Unto the swelling harmony
  Of the seraph angels' hymn.

And in that song of endless joy
  Mayst thou at last unite,—
When thy race on earth is run, fair boy,
  And thou hast gained the fight.
And in early life may thy Master see
  His armour girded on,—
Nor laid aside, until victory
  Proclaims the battle won !

Eva.

THE TRIALS OF LIFE.

" Is there no balm in Gilead?—is there no Physician there?"
JER. viii. 22.

Oh ! say while Life's broad stream is onward flowing,
    And each frail barque pursues the course unknown,
Is there to one a sky for ever glowing?
    Was there e'er one who told of joy alone !
No ! though around them airy visions floated,
    Though brightly may have dawned their early morn,
He—the All-righteous—hath in wisdom noted,
    " As sparks fly upwards, man to woe is born."

See where that wasted form in anguish glideth
    To one loved spot within the churchyard lone,
Craving for death, which now, alas ! divideth
    A widowed mother from her only son.
Yet, oh ! thou stricken mourner—broken-hearted,
    Childless and desolate, though thou mayst be—
Mourn not too deeply him who hath departed,
    For there is " balm in Gilead " still for thee.

And there an exile sad and lone is pining,
    Forced from his native land for aye to roam ;
Whilst many a fond remembrance round him twining.
    Brings to his mind his country and his home.

Ah ! lonely mourner, sad forsaken stranger,
　　There still is One who all thy woes can feel,—
Whose Hand will lead thee on through every danger,
　　And who thy griefs with " Gilead's balm " will heal.

See where that tall and haughty form is standing,
　　Of all his earthly goods at once bereft ;
Quenched is the fiery eye and glance commanding—
　　None of his boasted treasures now are left.
Yet, oh ! perchance this warning, timely given,
　　May loose the heart to earth so closely bound ;
And though each prospect fair from thee is riven,
　　There's " balm in Gilead " still for *every* wound.

Mark where that fair and youthful form is kneeling,
　　Who mourns her last and only parent gone ;
The tear of anguish down her cheek is stealing—
　　An orphan left in this bleak world alone !
Yet, though oppressed with sadness, care, and sorrow,
　　Friendless and fatherless although thou be,
Look for the dawning of a brighter morrow,
　　Still is there " balm in Gilead " poured for thee.

And there a husband, tears of madness weeping,
　　Deplores the loss of her,—his fondest pride,—
Who in her last " long home " is calmly sleeping,
　　While her first-born reposes by her side.
Yet, thou bereaved and lone one ! though around thee
　　Dark shadows rise, and cloud thy pathway o'er,
The chastening Hand which sent this grief to wound thee
　　Will ever " balm in Gilead " freely pour.

And thou, fair girl, whose eye upturned to Heaven,
   And quivering lip, the hidden woe bespeak,
I need not ask what tie from thee is riven,
   What untold agony now pales thy cheek.
Oh ! though thy "soul's first idol" hath forsaken,
   And clouded though thy brightest visions be,
Lift up the bleeding heart in faith unshaken,
   For there is " balm in Gilead" *e'en for thee !*

And thus we see where'er we look around us,
   That man is proved by sorrow from his birth ;
Some grief, in mercy, oft is sent to wound us ;
   Some stroke, perchance, to wean our souls from earth.
Then let us bow in humble, deep submission,
   With hearts resigned our every trial feel ;
For still "in Gilead" dwells the kind Physician,
   And He our deepest, bitterest woes will heal.

                          BEATRICE.

THE NEW YEAR.

ANOTHER year of Time's brief space gone by,-
   Another milestone of Life's journey past !
Here let me pause, and read with watchful eye
   The shadows by the light of Memory cast
O'er the departing scene, and thus receive
The lessons which that view is meant to give.

Yes ; there are shadows there—of sin, of doubt.
   Of trembling backwardness to do Thy will,
My best of friends ! a cloud of murmuring thought,
   Or vain desire, for what Thy mercy still
Withheld from one who *needs* Thy chastening rod,
   Lest she should wholly wander from her God.

But there is light as well ;—a precious gleam,
   Clothing the landscape with the hue of Heaven ;
Its focus is the Cross,—and in its beam
   I read the blessed tale of sin forgiven—
Help by the helpless found—the will subdued—
   And Peace, the purchase of a Saviour's blood.

Flowing within the soul, in those sweet hours
   When I have *felt* the joy of serving Thee ;—
Felt,—but too seldom !—Oh ! that all my powers
   May with this opening year more fully be
Upon Thine altar laid ; no more to move,
   But sweetly bound there by the cords of love.

AGNES.

DIRGE FOR THE OLD YEAR.

Farewell, eternally farewell to thee,
    Departed year !
With us no longer may thy dwelling be ;
    Our changing sphere
This night hath listened to the muffled tone
Which tells us that thy destiny is done.

The joys and sorrows it was thine to bring,
    When thou wast born,
Lie buried now beneath thy folded wing,
    Ne'er to return ;
Though many changes all around we see,
Which thou hast brought, but canst not take with thee.

To me how mournful sounds thy last farewell,
    Departed year !
For I have loved thy precious gifts so well,
    That o'er thy bier
'Tis meet the tear should fall, though all in vain ;
For thou art gone, and canst not come again !

Flowers, fair flowers, have sprung beneath thy tread,
    Whose fadeless bloom
A pure, undying fragrance long will shed
    Around thy tomb ;
That tomb from whose dark depths has risen now
A young, bright being, with unclouded brow.

Unclouded yet, though thunder-clouds may rise
   Around that form,
Which hath an untold mission from the skies
   Here to perform ;
And holds the fate of all the world beneath,
Alike the bearer both of life and death !

But 'tis not for our mortal eyes to gaze
   Within the veil ;
Though ofttimes would we that dim curtain raise,
   And learn the tale
Which the dark future hath recorded there—
Of new enjoyments, or unthought-of care.

Enough it is for our frail hearts to know
   He cannot err—
Who rules the hidden lot of all below ;—
   Then wherefore fear
The New Year's power to change our destinies,
Since " in the hollow of His Hand " it lies ?

Rather let Faith's clear eye be raised to Heaven,
   And read above,
That lessons both of grief and joy are given
   In boundless love,
To guide our spirits to that sinless shore,
Where " times and seasons " shall be known no more !

         Eva.

THE PAINTINGS OF THE HEART.

On ! thou who seekest by the light of Heaven
    For Nature's charms in wild luxuriance strewn ;
Who feelest that to other men is given
    A world of interest equal to thine own.

Dost thou not love in pensive mood to ponder
    Upon the treasures Art hath borne away ?
Through scenes that are no more, in thought to wander,
    Gazing on forms long passed into decay ?

Thou dost ! but nought thine eye is there beholding
    Can o'er thee rays so bright of pleasure dart,
As the deep things within thy soul unfolding—
    The strange mysterious paintings of the heart !

They are of scenes that meet thine eyes no longer ;
    Mountain and vale that once have felt thy tread ;
Spots that have watched the cords of love grow stronger,
    Whilst thought met thought, and kindly words were
        said.

In *them* are imaged forth thy childhood's hours,
    With all their vernal beauty quickly past ;
Bearing away from thee those radiant flowers
    Thou wouldst throughout thy future life to last

THE PAINTINGS OF THE HEART.

They have enshrined the absent ! unforgetting
    Thou lov'st each well-known feature to review ;
Till (lost in gladness, all thy vain regretting),
    Thou deem'st the *ideal* approaching to the true.

They give thee back from earth the long departed ;
    The deeply-loved, the deeply-mourned, are thine.
Gaze on them, till, no longer mournful hearted,
    Shalt thou at Heaven's high purposes repine.

They show the guardian spirits hovering o'er us—
    Perchance the friends that have been called away :
Who, past the bounded path that lies before us,
    Have found their home in realms of cloudless day.

Oh ! of *that home* thou hast some faint portraying
    Within the sacred chamber of thy soul ;
Though thick the mist thine earnest glances staying,
    Till Death shall bid its curtain upward roll.

IANTHE.

STANZAS.

"Oh! that I had wings like a dove! for then would I fly
away, and be at rest!"—Ps. lv. 6.

When sickness, care, and woe,
Teach us that man is ne'er supremely blest,
    How sweet it is to know
That earth is not our lasting place of rest.

    And not alone, when grief
Quells our affection for the things of time,
    Does the heart find relief
In turning to a brighter, happier clime.

    For when our hopes are high,
And the young heart sees nought but pleasure near,
    Still do we breathe a sigh
For bliss more perfect than awaits us here.

    Yes, while no clouds I see,—
While not a shadow dims the landscape bright,—
    Fain would my spirit flee,
And soar, unshackled, into realms of light.

Then are love's claims so small,
That I could part without a sigh or tear?
  How could I leave them all—
The dearly loved, the fondly cherished—here?

  Does not my panting heart
Shrink from a struggle it could scarcely bear?
  While longing to depart,
Yet cling to earth and all the treasures there?

  Oh! though the ties are strong
That chain me down below, and make me blest,
  More doth my spirit long
To reach a home of everlasting rest!

                                        BEATRICE.

FREDERICK VON SCHLEGEL

Was arrested by the hand of Death whilst preparing a lecture
on Knowledge; the last words he wrote being—" But the
consummate and the perfect knowledge——"

Oh, Death! thou mighty conqueror! mortal foe!
Whose fearful presence shades our path below,
    When will thy triumph end?
When is there, or when hath there been, the hour
That bids defiance to thy matchless power,
    To which all here must tend?

The bright, the beautiful, the best beloved,
By thy relentless hand are all removed,
    Far from their homes on earth.
" Rivers of sorrow " are called forth by thee,
One touch of thine can check the young heart's glee,
    And hush the voice of mirth.

When most unlooked for thou art at our door;
And what was yesterday is now no more—
    Borne on thy wings away.
Short though thy summons, yet it must be heard;
No prayers, no tears, can change thy changeless word,
    Or serve thy course to stay.

Mournfully solemn is thy conquest now,
Causing full many a loving head to bow
    Beneath the blow severe.

One has been severed by a moment's wing,
Just as his own heart's bright imagining
   Had reached its native sphere.

Unearthly radiance burned within his eye,
Which, as he raised it to the deep blue sky,
   Shone with a holy beam.
Bright thoughts, but rarely unto mortals known,
Poured on his spirit from the Eternal Throne,
   In a clear, blessed stream.

Then once again he bowed his noble head,
To tell the brightness that was o'er him shed,
   In one brief thrilling phrase ;
But the pure knowledge he had gained from Heaven,
To him—and unto him alone—was given,
   Ne'er to meet other gaze.

Pale and yet paler grew his lofty brow—
The light of genius is fading now
   At the cold touch of Death ;
The pen that quivers in his stiffening hand
Drops—as the summons from a far-off land
   Hushes the fleeting breath.

And he was gone ! his brilliant " sunset hour "
Came when his mind, in all its kindling power,
   Was bathed in light and bliss ;
A sweet foreknowlege of what was to come,
When he at last should reach his final home
   Of endless happiness !

" Perfect and consummate" thy knowledge *now*,
Bright, blessed dreamer ! snatched from all below
    In that thy hour of pride ;
When thou wert nearest to the longed-for goal,
And truth was dawning on thy earnest soul—
    Oh ! shouldst thou thus have died ?

It is not ours to say—thy work was done ;
Therefore the summons from the Almighty One
    Went quickly forth to thee.
In peace and joy thou listened to the word,
And bowed before the mandate of the Lord
    In calm serenity.

So the star vanished from our changing sky,
To beam with tenfold brilliancy on high,
    Where bright things never fade.
Oh ! when we feel, and know, that Terror's King
Bears such pure glory on his rapid wing,
    Would we that wing have stayed ?

Hasty the pinions that bore thee on ;
In one brief, breathless instant thou wert gone
    Over the black waves' foam.
Then angels welcomed thy triumphant flight,
And led thee to the land of life and light, —
    Thy everlasting home !

                            EVA.

THE BANK OF MOSS.

Whilst leafless trees and fading flowers were speaking
   of decay,
And haunting with their spectral forms an early
   winter's day,
A stony bank, by moss o'ergrown, with dewdrops
   sprinkled round,
Mid tiny rocks and mountains, a mimic forest crowned.
Now Fancy gazed upon the scene, and marked the dew-
   drops well ;
She deemed she saw the crystal halls wherein the
   fairies dwell :
Tales of their power in olden time passed o'er her mind
   again,
And she dreamed that they are wielding now the desti-
   nies of men.
Then Fancy—idle maiden—called her graver sister
   Thought,
To tell what visions to *her* mind the bank of moss had
   brought :
And Thought replied, "There is an hour that over men
   shall roll,
When flowers are dead, and skies are dull,—the winter
   of the soul ;—

G

They must not mourn their summer fled, but downward
  turn their eyes,
And mark what fair and lovely things in that dark time
  arise.
What though their lovely treasures with tears are
  sprinkled o'er,—
From out those crystal mansions ethereal spirits soar,—
Spirits whose strength is great to sway the stormy
  world within,—
Who help man to the victory o'er his opponent, Sin.
Thy fairy halls, my sister, will quickly pass away,
As the out-bursting sun proclaims the onward march of
  day ;
My crystal palaces must last till on the raptured sight,
The sun that cannot set shall rise,—an ' Everlasting
  Light !' "

            IANTHE.

"WHAT SHALL WE RENDER?"

Psalm cxvi. 12.

WHEN wintry winds around thy home are sweeping,
  And on thy casement beats the pelting storm,
When, like shut flowers, thy babes are calmly sleeping,
  Their soft cheeks nestled in their pillows warm ;
When on the parlour hearth the firelight glowing
  Seems but the brighter for the tempest-sound,
And Love's sweet presence at thy side, is throwing
  Its beams of joy and happiness around ;

Matron and mother ! whilst with humble gladness
  Thou musest on the mercies of thy lot,—
Is there not mingled oft a thought of sadness
  For those o'er whom such blessings blossom not ?
The homeless wanderer in the crowded city,
  The half-starved child who knows no fireside's gleam,
Does it not touch the deepest strings of pity
  To think what such a night must be for *them !*

What canst thou do to help them ?   'Twere not fitting
  To seek them out amidst the storm's wild roar ;
And yet across thy spirit, dimly flitting,
  Are there not yearnings to do something more !

                                             G. ?

More for the poor and helpless ! mutely pleading,
  Their sin and misery implore thine aid ;
Thou would'st not pass them by with step unheeding,
  When thus their woe upon thy heart is laid !

Maiden ! the tendrils of whose love are clinging
  So fondly unto those who gave thee birth,
As still in storm or calm their house is ringing
  With the clear music of thy girlish mirth ;
Oh ! spare a thought for those whose hearts are riven
  By care and anguish thou mayst never know ;
Like leaves before the winter tempest driven,
  Behold them,—perishing in want and woe !

Christian of England ! whilst with many a blessing
  Thy cup of life is by thy Father filled,
On thee a weight of stewardship is pressing,—
  Oh, may the solemn trust be well fulfilled !
If heavenly love upon thy heart is shining,
  Let thy poor neighbour read it mirrored there ;
If earthly flowers around thy home are twining,
  Should not their fragrance reach the haunts of care ?

Is there no purse that might at once receive them,—
  Some free-will offerings from thy full hands poured ?
And wilt thou not at Jesus' footstool leave them
  A tribute of thanksgiving to thy Lord ?
Now, lest with daylight and with calm returning,
  The secret purpose of thy heart give way,
And high resolves within thy spirit burning,
  Prove but a vapour,—vanishing away.

Channels there are through which thy bounty flowing,
 May reach and bless the lone and outcast poor ;
Others the pain and labour are bestowing ;
 They look to *thee* to help them from thy store.
Oh ! hear their strong appeal ! and sweetly blending
 The *work* of love with thoughts and words of praise,
Thou yet shalt find on heart and head descending
 A richer blessing through remaining days !

AGNES.

TEN YEARS TO COME.

Oh ! while a wreath of bliss is twined around us,
　And sorrow ne'er has marred our childhood's home,
How little do we know what griefs may wound us,
　What changes may be ours,—ten years to come ?

Ten years to come !—how many a heart now beating
　High in enjoyment of youth's careless mirth,
Its throbbing ceased,—may then be coldly sleeping
　In the last silent home of all the earth ?

Ten years to come !—the eye now brightly beaming
　With love, and joy, and radiance,—all its own,—
May then with sad and silent tears be streaming,
　Shed for the loved and lost,—too early flown.

Ten years to come !—the form at ease reclining,
　Where youth, and health, and grace, and beauty reign,
Then on the bed of sickness may be pining,
　Burning with fever, or oppressed with pain.

Ten years to come !—the youth now gaily speaking
　Of glowing scenes where he in fancy soars,—
May then, perchance, with aching heart, be seeking
　A home and fortune on far distant shores.

Ten years to come !—the maiden fondly thinking
   She ne'er was doomed to feel Affliction's smart,
Then 'neath a weight of sorrow may be sinking,—
   The withering sorrow of a wasted heart !

Ten years to come !—though now so bright before us
   The path of life may one of roses seem ;
How many a fearful cloud may then be o'er us,
   Changing the spirit of our early dream.*

Ten years to come !—oh ! many a mournful vision
   E'en now steals o'er my soul with saddening power ;
All-wise allotment ! merciful provision !
   That hides from man more than the passing hour.

                              BEATRICE.

* " A change came o'er the spirit of my dream."—BYRON.

THE FLOWERS' FAREWELL.

" WE are called, we are called from earth away :—
   Voices of music, breathing low,
With silvery accents around us say,—
   ' Lovely and loved ones,—ye must go !
For the gentle summer has hastened on
   In fair and far-off climes to dwell,
From her northern hamlet her smile is gone,
   Sweetly sighing a long farewell.

"And how can ye rest amid scenes of gloom,
   Where her voice will be heard no more ?
She has fondly smiled on your happy bloom—
   She is gone, and that bloom is o'er ;
And nought, fair flowers, can await you here
   But darkness and slow decay,
If ye linger still in this stormy sphere,—
   Ye are called, and ye must not stay !'"

Then the murmuring echoes sank to sleep,
   Hushed was that low and dreamy tone ;
And the lovely listeners turned to weep
   Over the summer so early flown.

But heavy and cold was the sparkling dew
   Resting upon their eyelids fair ;
And withered and wasted their beauty grew,
    Quickly seared in the autumn air.

And they knew that their home was not on earth,
   When winter neared to bind her brow ;
For the smiling sunbeams that gave them birth
   Ever seemed chill and cheerless now.
And the azure sky that rejoiced above,
   Laughing upon each bright young head ;
They were blessed no more with its glance of love—
   False and fickle, it too had fled.

Their welcome had thrilled in the untaught song
   Of full many a forest bird ;
They had listened now for that music long
   But no more might its voice be heard.
And the gentle zephyr, so soft and mild,
   That they danced to her tuneful breath—
She had mingled now with the tempest wild,
   As the bearer of blight and death.

Oh ! well may we see that this sin-fraught-clime
   Is no home for the bright and fair;
They are early called from the things of time
   To take flight into purer air.
How often our sweetest human flowers
   Are to make but an angel's stay ;
They gladden our paths through the summer hours.
   To be summoned too soon away.

From the bitter blasts of a wintry life
   They are called to a calmer home ;
And, ere yet hath commenced the weary strife,
   In Heaven those flowrets bloom.
To the mansions of peace and glory gone,
   Where perpetual summers reign ;
We may haste to them when our tasks are done,
   But they will not return again.

They have breathed adieu to their mortal birth,
   From the fetters of time set free ;
As brightly they bloomed in their homes on earth,
   They bloom on through eternity.
And their memory haunts the loving heart,
   Like the fair flowers' fading breath,
Whose lingering fragrance will ne'er depart,
   Nor grow faint 'neath the touch of Death.

                           Eva.

THE IDEAL.

THE Painter sits in his studio lone,
    When the gloom of night is round ;
On breathing canvass his glance is thrown,
    But a vacant spot is found ;
An outlined form that wants the soul
Which shall bear his work beyond Time's control.

The last sad hour's communion sweet *
    Of a band by friendship tried
His pencil pourtrays in colours meet,
    But great the task untried :
How paint *Him*—once on earth who trod —
Whose form was clay, whose soul was God ?

*   *   *   *   *

Hark ! waking the sleepy evening air,
    Is one whose soul is strong
In a strife from unseen worlds, to bear
    The spirit life of Song.
Ah ! to wind of earth will ne'er be given
To swell such strains as float in Heaven !

---

* In allusion to Leonardo da Vinci's celebrated painting of
the Last Supper.

When hurrying on in their swift career,
    The moments of night pass by,
Their whispers to dawn strike on thine ear,
    Oh, child of Melody !
And thou call'st to light on her rapid wing,
The harp of the morning stars to bring.

       *   *   *   *   *

The Poet awake in the starlight hour,
    When the tongue of day is still,
Feels a growing soul and a struggling power
    Through his mortal frame to thrill ;
The rush of a stream whose home must be
In the ocean of infinity !

Though now that stream hath a rocky shore
    To girdle its waters strong,
And a rugged channel it windeth o'er
    The depths of the heart along ;
It watches a calmer course to take,
When the vase at the fount of life shall break.

       *   *   *   *   *

Oh ! thou who feelest within thee spring
    A spirit that soars from clay—
Thou longest to rise on its eagle wing,
    From the mists of Time away ;
And, free from the fetters which earth must feel,
To grasp in truth thine own Ideal !

Yet e'en in this dreamy, shadowy land,
　　Thou mayst tune a string divine,—
Meet, when it drops from thy trembling hand,
　　In a harp of gold to shine ;
And the form that from earthly skill may flee,
The pencil of Heaven can paint on *thee !*

　　　　　　　　　　IANTHE.

THY LOOK OF LOVE.

WHEN sorrow darkens o'er my brow,
  And tears bedim mine eye,—
When earthly cares oppress me now,
  And clouds obscure my sky;
While, bound by Love's enthralling spell,
  My heart oft grief hath known,
One look can all my gloom dispel—
  Thy look of love, mine own!

When fast before me shadows fly,
  And grief no more is known,—
When tears no longer dim mine eye,
  And all my cares are gone;
Then, then, I hail that glance of thine
  I prize all else above;
For brighter joys but dimly shine
  Without thy look of love!

Thy look of love! it hath a power
  Far, far beyond aught else on earth,
To cheer when clouds of sorrow lower,
  Or brighter gild the hour of mirth.

What consolation sweet it is
　To mark those mild eyes beam on me,
Bringing the blessed consciousness
　That I am loved—and loved by *thee!*

Yes, so it is ; in smiles and tears,
　Alike that look I prize ;
And, oh ! whene'er in future years
　To view my failings rise,
Do thou, with kind and gentle art,
　My erring ways reprove ;
For, oh ! 't would almost break my heart
　To lose that look of love.

The kind rebuke of one so dear
　Will ne'er be heard in vain
By her who'll strive thy path to cheer,
　And thy approval gain :
And, oh ! her constant prayer will be
　That she may never prove,
My own beloved, unworthy thee,
　Nor of thy look of love !

BEATRICE.

LINES

ADDRESSED TO A YOUNG LADY, WHO, WATCHING THE
GLORIES OF A BRILLIANT SUNSET, EXCLAIMED, "OH !
THAT I HAD YON CLOUD FOR A CROWN !" *

SWEET buds may come from their woodland home
　　Around thy feet to bow ;
Thou mayst have bright flowers a few brief hours
　　To wreathe thy joyous brow.

Yet thou canst not rest ; and thy soul confessed
　　That it longed to bear from high
Yon cloud of gold,—oh ! aspirant bold,
　　Thou mayst not rob the sky !

While greets mine ear, in its glad career,
　　Thy voice of glee and mirth,
My spirit burns with thought that turns
　　To the future things of earth.

Life's fairest bowers are twined with flowers,
　　The blossoms of hope and love ;
I see them thine, on thy robe they shine,
　　And bloom thy brow above.

* Lydia II.—June, 1841.

Oh ! must they fade, and soon be laid
 Low in their native clay ?
What shall we give to bid them live
 Till death has passed away ?

Lift up thine eye ! there is a sky
 Whose glories man may share ;
Oh ! bright in hue, and rich in dew,
 The clouds are floating there.

Thy buds to save from an early grave,—
 Wouldst thou their treasures bear ?
Around Heaven's gate they stand and wait
 Upon the voice of prayer.

Dear one,—for thee, oh ! may there be
 Ere grief thy head has bowed,
'Mid gladsome hours, and fairest flowers,
 A crown of heaven-lit cloud !

IANTHE.

SAVIOUR! TO THEE I TURN.

Saviour ! to thee I turn ;
    My earthly heart would cease
From all its own imaginings,
    And come to Thee for peace.

Too often and too long,
My steps have wandered from th' appointed way ;
Now in the midst of weakness make me strong,
    And bid me no more stray !

I would be Thine, Thou know'st,—
I would cast out each sin, repel each foe,—
And, walking in Thy light, press forward still,
    Thy matchless love to know.

But, Lord, the work is Thine !
Weak, foolish, sinful, how can I withstand
The inward foes and outward snares which now
    Surround on every hand ?

Oh ! vain enquiry of my faithless heart,
When Thou Thy grace hast given
To strengthen my weak hands, subdue my sins.
    And lead me on to Heaven.

Forgive this unbelief,—
These doubts and fears which so becloud my way,
Reveal Thy glory to my waiting eyes,
    And change this night to day.

To Thee,—to Thee,—whose help
I have so oft in hours of darkness proved,
I would once more commit my soul,—by Thee
    Ransomed, and saved, and loved.

Oh, glorious hope !—oh, love unspeakable !
    Thy help will yet be near ;
The Comforter within my heart shall dwell,
    Thy love shall cast out fear !

And I shall praise Thee yet,—
With loosened tongue, and heart set free from care,
Shall know Thee reigning in this worthless heart,
    Making Thy temple there !

Not for *my* love, O Lord !
Who am but dust and ashes in Thy sight,—
But to *Thy* praise this rescue shall be wrought
    From sin, and Satan's might.

The work is Thine,—all Thine !
Oh ! let this thought my strength and comfort prove,
And may I humbly wait with prayer on Thee,
    'Till filled with all the riches of Thy love !
AGNES.

STANZAS.

The following lines were suggested by an anecdote in the Introduction to "Rob Roy," concluding in the following words:—"He never could forget the intense cold of that night, insomuch that in the bitterness of his heart he cursed the bright moon for giving no heat with so much light."

Ah ! such is Life,—with brightest hues now glowing,
　　All wreathed in gems and flowers ;
While a clear stream of light around us flowing
　　Leads us to dream of life-reviving powers,—
Till oh ! deceived,—we curse the world for showing
　　The semblance, only,—ours.

And such is Man !—whose brow all bright appeareth,
　　Open, and free from care,—
But cold and sad is oft the heart that weareth
　　Garment so bright and fair ;
We look for warmth, and joy soon disappeareth
　　If *light* alone is there.

And when young Love with glittering wreath has
　　　　crowned us,
　　The heart with rapture glows ;
We dream not of the power he hath to wound us,
　　'Till oft he shows
'Tis but the light of love now flickering round us,
　　Which yet no warmth bestows.

But oh ! a truer light there is revealed us,
　　Less dazzling though its gleam ;
We own its cheering power to guide and shield us,
　　And bless its sunny beam ;
Religion's light alone true warmth can yield us
　　On life's dark stream.

Then come, ye weary ones, whose hearts are yearning
　　For scenes than earth more bright,
And to that land your trembling footsteps turning,
　　Where there is " no more night,"—
Behold the Lamp of Love serenely burning,
　　Which yields both warmth and light !

　　　　　　　　　　　　　BEATRICE.

FAREWELL TO EASTWOOD.*

Farewell ! a long, a last farewell, my bright and early
    home,—
Farewell to all thy loveliness, thy sweet and verdant
    bloom ;
Oh ! Earth has many sunny spots, but none again can
    prove
The birthplace of such tender ties,—such deep, devoted
    love !

And must it be that thou wilt pass like thy swift
    Severn's tide,
To be a stranger's dwelling-place,—to be a *stranger's*
    pride ?
Yes,—all too vainly may the tears of yearning fondness
    flow,—
The mournful fiat has gone forth,—thou *art* another's
    now !

Though chequered years have passed away since those
    gay, joyous hours,
When last we wandered through thy shades, or culled
    thy gem-like flowers,—

---

* Eastwood, Portishead : the early home of the writer,
and built by her father.

Not yet has time unlinked the chain that bound thee to
    each heart,—
No! prized and loved as thou wert then,—far dearer
    now thou art!

Dearer to me,—although perchance some others may
    forget
The sun-bright home of early years,—oh! *I* will love
    thee yet;
Though other ties are forming fast, still slight their
    bonds must be,—
For I long to burst them all, and fly across the main to
    thee!

And as I mount the grassy hill to have one yearning
    gaze
At the spot where thou art standing forth, far o'er the
    distant waves,—
A wild, fierce hatred burns my soul, to think that I am
    here,
To think I thus am kept from thee,—from all my "heart
    holds dear!"

But softer, sadder feelings rise, as I catch thy shadowed
    form,
Standing in such calm beauty on, through sunshine and
    through storm,
And I dare not murmur at the Hand which placed me
    here to dwell,
The hand of One who cannot err,—who doeth all things
    well!

Then teach me, oh, Thou Perfect One ! to bow in trust
      to Thee,
Nor let such bitter thoughts arise at this thy just
      decree ;
Teach me to tear my heart-roots up where they are
      clinging yet,
And in Thy mercy and Thy truth,.oh ! let that heart
      forget !

Nor fix again such fervent love on any earthly home,—
Where perfect peace and perfect rest can never,—never,
      come,—
But strive to read its " title clear" to the home which
      may be given,
If sought with prayer and contrite faith, in the pure,
      bright realms of Heaven !

                                         Eva.

LINES

SUGGESTED BY OBSERVATIONS ON THE HARSH MANNER
IN WHICH PROFESSING CHRISTIANS SPEAK OF EACH
OTHER'S FAULTS.

WE judge of others when mirth hath spread
    Its glittering mantle o'er them,
And their idle words have swiftly fled
    To dim the path before them.

When Satire's shaft hath taken wing,
    Some shrinking bosom paining ;
And the wounds from Anger's venomed sting
    The mental page are staining.

We judge them when Thought her golden throne
    In heedless sport is leaving ;
And hearts that the Spirit of Heaven would own.
    Their sacred Friend are grieving.

We are not by when their bitter tears
    From eyes o'ercharged are flowing,—
Upon the graves of their by-gone years
    A stream of grief bestowing.

We see them not when the struggling soul
  In voiceless prayer is rising,
O'er floods of passion that mock control,
  From aught of man's devising.

We heed not the strife in its fierce career
  Through minds too oft despairing ;
But, oh ! when the victors, triumphant here,
  Their boughs of palm are bearing,—

When angel eyes shall gladly mark
  The arms of Love enfold them, ·
In the land where skies no more are dark—
  Say, shall *we* there behold them ?

                                        IANTHE.

THE LANGUAGE OF MUSIC.

SWEET sounds were ringing through a lofty room,
   Rising and falling on the summer air,
When in the zenith of her spring-like bloom,
   Rousing the melody that floated there,
A maiden sat, whose light and fairy touch,
Called forth the harmony we loved so much,
And gave it quenchless beauty.   Full and clear
      The gushing notes burst forth—
     The language of a distant sphere
     Re-echoed down to earth.
     Exulting on its magic way,
      The thrilling tune flows on,
     With nought to interrupt the sway
      Of each impetuous tone.
Oh ! therefore cease that bright-bewitching strain,
Painting proud visions all too false and vain—
Kindling wild feelings soon to die again !

A soft, sweet melody is breathing now,
The melting music of that voice is low,
And rich, and clear—it speaks of calmer things.
Gentler the phantoms which its pure tone brings
Into the troubled heart, and deep and still
Is feeling's tide ; but soon that tide must fill,—

And fill to overflowing—'neath the power
    Of this resistless stream,
Which makes the past a burning hour,
    The future all a dream—
A lovely dream of peace and bliss
    Centred in earthly happiness.
It tells of all that makes life's span
    So dazzling and so fair ;
And it tempteth frail and erring man
    To fix his treasure there !

And it pierces e'en the caverns deep
    Of woman's trusting breast,
Waking the passioned thoughts that sleep
    In that, their home of rest.
And sweetly, strangely, her soul is bowed,
    With a weight she would not move,
As visions of beauty round it crowd,
    Gilded and sunned by Love !
But hush ! the spell must cease,—it breaks too far
    Into the spirit's yet unfathomed sea,—
Enough for this weak life the things that *are ;*
While those that are not, and can never be,
Oh ! say—should *they* be fraught with such intensity ?

I listen once again ; and sad and slow
    The tones are pealing forth,—
I deem the voice of Music telleth now
    Of other things than earth ;
Yes,—'tis the death-note sounding through the air,
    In solemn cadences it murmurs there !

The master-hand* at whose sure touch it rose,
  E'en as he neared the tomb,—
Is resting now in dreamless, deep repose
  Far in his final home ;
Well may the latest flash from Genius given,
Have in its brightness less of earth than heaven !
And as the clear note of the dying swan
  Grows sweeter as his life is ebbing fast,
With mournful melody this strain flows on,—
  The purest,—loveliest,—because the *last !*
No earth-born thoughts may live beneath its spell,
No fruitless day-dreams 'midst its beauties dwell ;
No earnest longings for what may not be,
Its blessed language speaks *reality !*
Solemn the meaning of that muffled breath,
That quivers o'er us like the voice of Death,
Until subdued by some clear tone that brings
Visions of higher and more glorious things ;
The rich inheritance that waits above,
For those who've trusted in a Saviour's love ;
The crown celestial that fadeth not,
The unseen—untold beauty of that spot,—
The welcome haven of Life's restless sea,—
The endless joys of Immortality—
Music,—sweet Music ! thus thou speak'st to me !

Eva.

---

* " Weber's Last Waltz " is the air alluded to.

THE OASIS.

Sad men their way are slowly making
 O'er burning wastes of sand ;
Rich in gold the stores they're taking
 Through Afric's weary land :
Hark ! to the strains of song awaking
 From lips in that careworn band.

  " Brethren ! a toilsome path
   Day after day is ours,
  Sahara's desert hath
   Nor fruits, nor smiling flowers.

  We see but sand and sky ;
   Green shrubs and trees no more
  Refresh the aching eye,
   The wearied frame restore.

  Oft with a fearful rush,
   The scorching simoom's breath
  Our murmuring tongues would hush,
   And make them still in death.

  Or, in a fatal hour,
   Huge moving pillars haste,
  O'erwhelming mortal power,
   Beneath the sandy waste ;

As when wild breezes swell
  The blue sea's restless wave,
And mounting billows tell
  Of many an ocean grave.

Brethren ! we well may weep
  Rivers of sorrow here ;
Yet see,—your courage keep,—
  Yon green oasis near.

Oh ! bright and blessed isle !
  Our hearts were near to die ;
Yet once again we smile,
  As we behold thee nigh !"

How would the fainting and weary-hearted
  Each haste to that fertile spot,—
Joy o'er the woes for awhile departed,
  And rest in their peaceful lot,—
Till in their onward journey started,
  They find it their home is not.

And how to high Allah's temple thronging,
  Would their mingling voices raise
Unto his ear, the meed belonging
  Of earnest, heartfelt praise,—
From souls that for ceaseless bliss are longing,
  When ended their earthly days.

    *   *   *   *   *   *

Are not *our* weary footsteps failing
    In a sad and barren land,
To bless our path no more availing
    Than the waste of desert sand ?
And are we the bright oases hailing
    Dispensed by our Father's hand ?

Six days doth the sun behold us pining
    'Mid the golden stores amassed,—
Our souls to passions fierce resigning,
    As to the simoom's blast ;
But glory greets his *seventh* outshining,
    And our toils awhile are passed !

Hail to thy shores, thou isle of blessing !
    We pant for the green plains there,—
Clear waters to quench our thirst distressing,
    And rest from our load of care ;
Then may we, the goodness of Heaven confessing,
    Rejoice in the house of prayer.

Yes, let us raise our voice decided,
    To Him our homage pay,—
In whose changeless love have the souls confided
    Who know but *one* Sabbath day ;
Adoring the Hand which has thus provided
    Oases to cheer our way !

                          IANTHE.

TO MY DEPARTED FATHER.

" The memory of the just is blessed."—PROV. x. 7.

My honoured parent ! years have rolled away,
   Bearing me with them down the stream of time,
Since thy freed spirit left its house of clay,
   To dwell for ever in that blessèd clime,
Where the redeemed their Saviour's power adore,
And sin, and pain, and death, are known no more.

But still how freshly in remembrance dwell
   The incidents that marked thy closing days !
How memory lingers o'er the fond farewell,—
   The words of love, the kiss, the warm embrace :
Which from the fulness of thy heart were shed,—
A parting blessing on thy daughter's head !

I left thee then in health ; but sickness soon
   Had prostrate laid thy loved and honoured head ;
And, in the stillness of thy hallowed room,
   Thy wife and children gathered round thy bed,
To watch, with sorrowing hearts, the parting strife.
Which we call death. but which to thee brought life.

I

The dawn of life above ! words were not given—
   They were not needed in that solemn hour.
To tell us of thy humble hope of Heaven—
   Thy trust in the Redeemer's love and power.
Long had thy footsteps trod the narrow way—
We knew it led thee to eternal day.

I would not call thee from that blessèd home
   To tread again earth's paths of grief and pain ;
Though oft a yearning o'er my spirit come,
   And in my heart a vacant place remain.
Whilst vainly does the longing wake to prove
Once more the shelter of a father's love !

Vainly ! Oh, word of unbelief ! whilst He
   Whose mercy on the fatherless descends,
'Neath His own wing so oft hath sheltered me,
   And proved Himself the tenderest, best of Friends ;
Guiding in darkness, shielding from all ill—
Leading my trembling footsteps onward still !

Oh, no—not vainly ! Father, could thine eyes
   Look down to earth, and now thy child behold,
How would a louder song of praise arise
   To Him who led the wanderer to His fold ;
And washed, and healed, and bid her no more rove,
But with His flock, worship, and feed, and love !

And now though sorrow o'er my heart oft darken,
   And sin remaining, cost me many a tear,—

I would but seek more earnestly to hearken
    To His commands, and follow Him whilst here :
Trusting His power and love to carry on
The work which His free mercy hath begun.

And, oh, my Father ! that we all may meet,
    Thou and thy loved ones in that glorious Home,-
Where, worshipping around our Saviour's feet,
    No sound of sin or grief shall ever come :
But every brow His holy name shall bear,
And every countenance his likeness wear !

AGNES.

THE REALITIES OF LIFE.

ADDRESSED TO IANTHE (THE WRITER'S SISTER .

OH ! canst thou blame me that my tears are streaming,
  My heart's gay sunshine veiled in sadness now ?
As first it wakes from youth's bright, careless dreaming,
  'Tis meet that grief should darken o'er my brow,—
I would not pass this mournful era by
With undimmed spirits bounding joyously.

I have been happy : for the name of sorrow
  Is all, as yet, that hath been known to me ;
The gliding onward of each cloudless morrow,
  Did not unveil one stern reality ;
In dreams and phantasies my youth has passed,—
But they are over—life is come at last !

And gone for ever is the fair illusion,
  That earthly joy brings *peace* upon its wing ;
No longer guided by the "dear delusion,"
  I turn from my blind heart's imagining ;
From the bright hopes so fondly nursed by me,
  For now I feel them only vanity !

Oh ! I have hoped to find more cloudless pleasure,
  Delight more pure than mortal e'er may know ;
A home and resting-place for heart and treasure,—
  And willingly they both were fixed below ;

While yet the gorgeous curtain floated free,
Concealing Life's realities from me.

But it was raised at last ; I sat one even,
    Trembling and awe-struck by Death's solemn bed ;
The sun was sinking in the western heaven,
    Thrice more to rise upon that youthful head,—
And then for her the fevered strife was done,—
To peace and purity her soul was gone.

Oh ! had her days passed gaily and unheeded,
    An awful portion hers might then have proved ;
But not one fear for that calm soul was needed,—
    She loved her Saviour,—was by Him beloved ;
And so He called her in her sunny prime,
To part for ever from the things of Time.

And brightly thus her young life fled before us,
    With low prayers sounding in her dying ear
To spare the blow so darkly pending o'er us ;
    Oh ! they were breathed for *us*—but not for *her !*
Her faint breath fluttered—and her eye grew dim,
Her Lord received her,—she is now with Him !

Could I forget her ?—she was with me ever,—
    Both night and day her form would haunt my brain ;
Moments there are which come in life,—but never
    Depart to leave our hearts the same again !
Such were those moments when I saw her last ;
Years will roll onward ere their power is passed.

*   *   *   *   *   *

Changed was the scene ; upon a couch reclining,
  Waiting her summons, a fair creature lay,—
And quickly too was her loved life declining,
  As dread Consumption firmly grasped his prey :
But in calm beauty still she lingered on,—
A holy, lovely sight to look upon.

A strengthening lesson to the weak and wounded :
  A word of warning to the young and gay ;
In life's glad morn, with constant health surrounded,
  E'en they may soon—too soon—be called away.
So conscience whispered, as the sad eye gazed
On that sweet rosebud ere its bloom decayed !

Her cheek was fading,—but her eye was beaming
  With a clear light from Heaven all radiant there :
No more the tears for sin and sorrow streaming
  Again shall glisten 'neath her eyelids fair :
Oh ! none could wish her now to linger here,
Not even those who hold her life most dear.

Yet who could wander 'mid such scenes of sadness,
  Making an entrance into life's wild grief,—
Nor feel that what once caused light-hearted gladness,
  Now failed to bring the aching heart relief ?
So first comes o'er the soul the truth forlorn,
" As sparks fly upwards, man to woe is born !"

But all alike may learn the truth consoling,
  That the stern smiter is the kindest friend ;
He guides the thunder-clouds around us rolling,
  And p urest comfort will, if sought for, send :

Shows us that " weeping may endure a night,"
But "joy" shall come e'en with the " morning" light !

But for the thought that He is ever near us,
   How could we meet the bitter storms of life ?
Without His changeless love to guard and cheer us,
   And aid our spirits in the weary strife ?
Oft should we sink beneath the tempest's power,
O'erwhelmed and fainting in each stormy hour.

How could we bear the pangs of vainly loving ?
   The blanks of Death, as the dread arrow flies ?
Some object of our fondest hopes removing, --
   The sternest of life's stern realities !
Absence and change,—sickness and early blight, -
Would not these shroud us in an endless night ?

Then thanks to Him who hath in mercy given,
   Bright beams to cheer us like the summer sun ;
Thanks to the King of Kings,—the Lord of Heaven,
   For all He does,—and all He leaves undone !
His Arm will guide us in our chequered way,
Till night has yielded to Eternal Day !

EVA.

THE LIVING WATER.

" Whosoever drinketh of the water that I shall give him, shall
never thirst."—JOHN iv. 13.

DOST thou oft feel alone ?
And midst the earthly blessings that surround thee,
Hath not thy Father with that sweet gift crowned thee,
   A heart that beats in union with thy own ?

One daily by thy side,
From whom thy joys an added light should borrow,
Whose smile should cheer thee in the hour of sorrow,-
   At once a friend, a helper, and a guide !

Belovèd ones there are,—
Dear ties of kindred, oft thy pathway brightening,
And many a load of care and sorrow lightening,
   Which with their loving spirits thou canst share ;

But one thou lackest still,
Whose bosom throbs with a responsive feeling
To the same notes, which o'er thy spirit stealing,
   Its inmost chords of joy or sorrow thrill.

Lift thy sad heart above,
Christian! and grieve not that thy lot is lonely,—
If He who died, and lives to bless thee,—only
    Remembers thee in His unchanging love.

Is He not always nigh,—
With tender sympathy each rough path smoothing?
Sharing thy joy, and thy worn spirit soothing,—
    Watching thee ever with His pitying eye!

Yes! and His heart of love
Well knows the depth of that mysterious yearning,
With which the spirits He has formed are burning,—
    Ever some fuller sympathy to prove.

But He would have them *now*,—
These tendrils of thy heart,—round Him so clasping.
That, earth's vain hopes and joys no longer grasping,
    Thou the full bliss of *love* indeed may'st know!

All thou canst safely bear,
He freely gives thee of terrestrial blessing:
But thou a higher heritage possessing,
    Must learn to *centre* thy affections there.

And if with pain oppressed,—
Anguish of parting, loneliness of feeling,—
'Tis but to draw thee to His feet for healing,
    To teach thee sweetly upon Him to rest.

Then be thy yearnings stilled !
And praise His love who only sends thee sadness,
That from the well-spring of eternal gladness
    Thy thirsting heart may evermore be filled.

    Let every idol fall,—
Wait on His will with love's sweet resignation,—
So shalt thou find in Him thy full salvation,—
    Jesus, thy Saviour, shall be all in all !

                                AGNES.

STANZAS.

How oft, when all without seems fair,
  The heart with grief is torn,
And they *we* think most happy are
  Those who the deepest mourn.

And when the brow of youth appears
  Decked in its gayest smile,—
How oft the *heart* is full of cares
  And sorrow all the while!

BEATRICE.

LAST HOURS AT BRYMBO.*

Oh ! tell me wherefore are the sunny hours
    So short and swift to-day ?
I see them decked with all earth's fairest flowers,
    And yet they will not stay,—
But, lightly scattering their fairy showers,
    They speed away—away !

Oh ! pause ye bright ones on your rapid wings,
    Nor hasten on so fast,—
Why are the bearers of such glorious things
    No sooner come than past ?
Tenfold the beauty that each wanderer brings,
    Too rich—too pure to last !

It may not be,—still onward,—onward,—going,
    I mark your hasty flight,—
Whose wingèd speed is far too plainly showing
    How frail is all that's bright !
Short-lived the roses in your sunshine growing ;
    They each must fade to-night !

        —

* The home of an intimate friend of the writer.

For on the morrow will your portion be
　　　To bear me far away
From this sweet home of mirth and revelry,
　　　So doubly dear to-day ;
Fain would I linger 'mid such scenes of glee,
　　　Oh ! let me, let me stay !

You hearken not,—but moving, ever moving,
　　　Each rising hope you quell ;
The steady haste of those fleet pinions proving
　　　Clearly as words could tell,—
How soon I now must breathe to loved and loving
　　　A long,—a last farewell !

I look around me ;—smiles are brightly glancing,
　　　As the gay jest is passed,—
And every heart, *save one*, is lightly dancing,—
　　　One brow alone o'ercast ;
Why should *she* mourn the evening hours advancing !
　　　That evening is her *last !*

Her last at Brymbo !—yet she scorns to borrow
　　　One pang from future pain ;
To feel to-day what *must* be felt to-morrow
　　　Is all alike in vain ;
Depart then quickly, ye dark shades of sorrow :
　　　Ye bright thoughts, come again !

And give me courage to "hope on, hope ever,"
 E'en through the deepest gloom,
To press on joyously,—despairing never,
 Of what is yet to come ;—
The bursting of these ties so hard to sever,
 Will only bear me—*home!*

The "place of rest" for woman,—whose fond soul
 Turns from the storms of life,
When o'er those storms she can have no control.
 To calm or quell their strife ;
She shrinks to hear the tempest's ceaseless roll,
 With noisy tumult rife.

And though all-dazzling are the pleasures. springing
 Where restless spirits dwell,—
I dread the enchantments they are round me flinging,
 And must resist the spell ;
Nor to their fearful radiance wildly clinging,
 Regret the word - " Farewell ! "

For it will lead me to a calmer spot,
 Less dangerous,—more dear ;
Where, midst the duties of a peaceful lot,
 A quiet, noiseless sphere,
Will, unlamented be,—though not forgot,—
 The burning brightness *here !*

And now to rest—I hear the brief command.
  I see the taper's light.—
How warm the pressure of the " iron hand ;"
  The farewell smile is bright ;—
Well may I hasten to Oblivion's land,—
  Good-night, kind friends, good-night !

           Eva.

LEYLA.

A TALE FOUNDED ON FACT.

" The Parsees of Bombay (who may very justly be called
the Quakers of the East), though an enlightened and humane
tribe, possess many singular customs, and strict and regular
usages; one of these is the obligation to marry only within
the tribe. Any aberration from this practice is punished
with immediate death, and nothing can avert the fate of the
unfortunate victim."—*Tales and Sketches of a Soldier's Life.*

IT was an eve of silent loveliness,—
    Nature is hushed in still and calm repose ;
Proud vessels on the wave lie motionless,
    And all around in tranquil beauty glows,
Where, fanned by many a perfume-scented breeze,
Lies a fair island 'midst the Indian seas.

'Twas when the sun's last rays all brightly shone
    Upon the waves that wash thy shore, Bombay.
That, wrapt in thought, unheeded and alone,
    In musing solitude a maiden lay ;
Her tearful, restless eye, and varying cheek,
Some mighty struggle of the soul bespeak.

Oh ! she was beautiful ! her clear dark eye
    Now shed its soft and smiling light around ;
And now, as sudden clouds obscure the sky,
    Was fixed in mournful gaze upon the ground ;

So earnest and so sad, you well might deem
Her memory lingered on some fearful dream.

Her long black tresses fell around her now
   In simple beauty, decked with pearls alone ;
Scarce sixteen years had passed across her brow,
   Yet those mild eyes, so full of light, that shone,
Told that within young Leyla's lofty mind,
All woman's holiest feelings lay enshrined.

She was her Father's loved and only child,
   Heiress to wealth he had with care amassed ;
Full oft his tedious hours had she beguiled,
   And chased the cloud as o'er his brow it passed.
Thus loving and beloved, her days had flown,
Whilst her young heart had scarce a sorrow known.

But ah ! how seldom 'tis our lot to dwell
   Amid the pleasures youth's gay visions bring :
No longer Leyla's heart could own the spell
   That flung such brightness round her early Spring :
A shade was resting on that marble brow,
That told she knew of care and sorrow *now!*

Yes, for a youth who from afar had come,
   Won by her beauty, sought her as his bride :
Implored her now to leave that cherished home,
   And claim him only as her guard and guide.
Urged her to fly to Britain's happy shore,
Where nought but death should ever part them more.

K

All warmly proffered was that gallant heart ;
   And soon had Leyla fixed her ardent love—
The love that only can with life depart—
   On him she idolized all else above :
Oft did they meet, and 'neath the starry heaven,
Their vows of changeless constancy were given.

Full well her tribe's decree the maiden knew,
   To all who dare those changeless laws defy ;
And as that fearful doom now rose to view,
   The tear-drop trembled in her downcast eye ;
Fierce were the struggles that her bosom wrung,
And o'er her brow their darkening shadow flung.

She thought upon her father's wild despair,
   When thus forsaken by his only child ;
She thought upon her mother weeping there,
   Who oft so tenderly on her had smiled ;
And shrank with horror from the early tomb,
Which she too sadly feared might be her doom.

But then her heart, with "love's true instinct," turned
   To him who would have died her life to save ;
Each wavering feeling from her soul she spurned,
   All, *all* her terrors to the winds she gave,
E'en thoughts of death no longer fear impart,
Love was the victor in that youthful heart !*

---

  * " *Thou* art the victor, Love !"—*Mrs. Hemans.*

With high resolve marked on her gentle brow,
   In queen-like majesty, the maiden rose;
To her loved home she turns her footsteps now,—
   Strength more than mortal in her bosom glows :
The fear—the " bitterness "—of death is past,
And Leyla's destiny is fixed at last !

    *   *   *   *   *   *

They fled !—upon their steeds of fiery might,
   Ere morning dawned, they sped their rapid way ;
Scarce had day yielded to the gloom of night
   Ere that fair girl a mourning captive lay.
Three armed pursuers followed in their track,
With stern command to bring the victim back.

Wildly and nobly fought the gallant youth,
   From their rude grasp that gentle girl to save ;
Flashed o'er his soul the dark and maddening truth,
   That for *his* sake she'd find an early grave ;
But soon exhausted with his wounds he lay,
While Leyla from his sight was borne away.

    *   *   *   *   *   *

The scene is changed. Within a lofty room,
   Where all the elders of her tribe are seen,
Waiting undauntedly to hear her doom,
   A maiden stands with high and haughty mien :—
'Tis Leyla's form, and Leyla's flashing eye,
That calmly marks this mournful pageantry !

                                K 2

Arrayed in costly robes of bridal hue,
    While glittering jewels deck her youthful form,—
Unmoved, unyielding, to her nature true,—
    She proudly stood, unscathed amidst the storm.
An hour it was of dark and dread despair,
But woman's dauntless courage triumphed there !

Firmly she breathed to all a last farewell,
    Then from her mother took the fatal bowl ;
No tear of sadness from her eyelid fell,
    No yielding softness o'er her bosom stole :—
She drained the cup—soon drooped her gentle head—
The fair, the bright, the beautiful, was dead !

And when her sad and cruel fate was known
    To him for whom that hapless maiden died,
Reason no longer could maintain her throne ;
    He urged his courser to the foaming tide :—
One speck a moment darkened o'er the main,
And Leyla's lover ne'er was seen again !

                                        BEATRICE.

THE SABBATH.

"For a day in thy courts is better than a thousand."
PSALM lxxxiv. 10.

OH ! all too soon thy golden hours fleet by,
Sweet day of holy rest ! which seems to bring
My thirsty spirit nearer to that fount
Whose streams "make glad the city of our God."
I love thy blessed calm,—thy hallowed peace,—
Coming like dew upon the waiting soul,
To make a Sabbath there, and bid it press
With quickened ardour towards that heavenly rest,
Which "yet remaineth" for the child of God,—
Where sin and grief are not.   Oh ! may I then,
As each succeeding Sabbath dawns upon me,
With humble watchfulness still wait on Him
From whom all blessings come ; and thus receive
From His full hand renewal of my strength,
Help in the time of need, and every gift
Which, in the riches of His grace and love,
He willingly bestows on all who come
In humble faith to Him !

AGNES.

LINES

SUGGESTED BY SEEING A TREE BEARING FRUIT AND
FLOWERS AT THE SAME TIME, WHICH IS SAID TO BE
A SIGN OF DEATH.

SADNESS and care a youthful brow are veiling,
  And shadows come where sunshine used to be ;
" Wherefore the troubled gaze, the bright cheek paling,
  Is life so joyless then, fair girl, to thee ?"

" Yes—life *is* joyless—for the mournful feeling,
  The strange vague sense of sorrow yet to come,
By night, by day, across my heart is stealing,
  Shrouding its joys beneath a dreary gloom.

" For oh ! I hear in low, mysterious murmur
  The voice of Death in every breeze that sighs ;
Vainly my soul has struggled to be firmer
  Phantoms of terror still around it rise.

" Unearthly visions ever float before me,
  Unearthly voices fill the summer air ;
What is the unseen doom thus pending o'er me ?
  Whence is the weary weight, so hard to bear !

" Omens and signs seem all alike portending
   That grief is hovering near me and around ;
Darkening the present, to the future lending
   A depth of dread my weak heart dare not sound.

" I see pale flowers the trees of earth adorning,
   And midst their bloom the rich fruit ripens fast ;
While to each thoughtful spirit comes the warning
   That this fair season is perchance the last.

" That ere another summer dawns in gladness,
   The grave may open to receive its dead ;
And o'er our loving hearts a night of sadness,
   ' That knows no morrow,' shall for aye be spread.

" And that small thing—Death's watcher, now is making
   Its low quick signal on our household walls ;
Nor there alone—for on my sad heart aching,
   That thrilling sound with mournful power falls.

" And Death, I deem, on rapid wings is coming
   The swift and solemn herald of the tomb—
To watch the last sands in the hour-glass running,
   Of some beloved one, who is nearing home.

" Then marvel not that with such dark foreboding
   The sparkling fount of girlhood's joy should fail ;
Its bright stream poisoned with fears so corroding,
   My smile must sadden, and my cheek grow pale."

" And hast thou then no trust, nor faith confiding
   In Him without whose leave no sparrow dies ?
Thou yet must learn that those in Him abiding
   Seek not to read the future's mysteries.

" But humbly strive to do their *present* duty,
   And leave the morrow to His gracious care ;
So life to them is full of joy and beauty
   For His protecting love is always there !

" Though heart and flesh may fail, and footsteps quiver.
   Safe in that love the weakest can recline ;
Small room for fear, where peace flows like a river :
   Pray thou that such peace may henceforth be thine !"

EVA.

DEATH.

"And the Angel of Death spread his wings on the blast."—
BYRON.

"SPIRIT OF TERROR! stay thy rapid wing,
    A moment pause in this thy dread career ;
Tell me to whom thou flies this day, to bring
    The fatal hour that ends their pleasure here."

" As ever, child of earth, will be my flight,
    And vain it is to ask to whom I go ;
'Tis yours to bow beneath my changeless might,
    But of the ' days and hours shall no man know.'

" Yet though I may not my dark mission tell,
    Thou canst in thought its gloomy course attend.
Conceive the spirit bidding earth farewell,
    And entering on the world that knows no end.

" To some arrayed in mournful garb I come ;
    Perchance undreamt of 'mid gay scenes below,
I summon them to their eternal home,—
    Against me strive they may,—but they *must* go."

" Where is that home ?"   " Thou canst not pierce
        the shade
    Veiling its deathless horror from thine eye ;
Thou canst not see the guilty soul conveyed
    To its abode of quenchless agony.

"Oh ! suffer not thy heart too close to cling
  To glorious visions it may here behold ;—
Clasp not too fondly life's most cherished thing,
  Though round it brightest flowers of earth unfold.

"Yet are there some who do not dread my voice,
  Nor startle at the rustling of my wing,—
Whose echoing spirits at the sound rejoice,
  And haste their God's immortal praise to sing."

"Where is *their* home ?" "They are the robed in white,
  Whose eyes shall weep no more before the throne,
To whom the sun shall cease to give his light,
  And the pale moonshine be no longer known.

"From sin and sorrow freed, they find their rest,
  Where my dark pinions shall be seen no more ;-
In that calm land,—the home of spirits blest,—
  My triumphs of a moment shall be o'er."

IANTHE.

DEATH.

"There is no discharge in that war."—ECCLES. viii. S.

How shall I die?—how oft that question thrilling,
  Has pressed with solemn weight upon my soul,
When I have sought to trace with trembling feeling,
  Some parted spirit onward to its goal ;
That goal of endless joy,—or woe unknown,
That waits us all when life's brief course is run.

Must I, too, bear those pangs of mortal anguish,
  By which the veil of flesh is often rent ?
Or through protracted months of weakness languish,—
  Or in a moment hear the summons sent !
Which comes a voice of terror unto some,—
To others a sweet welcome to their home !

Yes ! in that fearful warfare no discharging
  Can from the conflict give the power to flee ;
For the grave still, its boundaries enlarging,
  A place prepares for each,—for all,—for thee.
Thou knowest not how—thou knowest not when ; but yet
Thou and this awful foe must surely meet !

Yet why these fears ? If on thy Lord relying,
　　His blood thy hope,—His cross thy refuge,—know
For thee remaineth but the name of dying ;
　　He whom thou fearest is a conquered foe,
Whose utmost power can only set thee free,
With thy Redeemer evermore to be.

Jesus hath trod the shadowy vale before thee,
　　His arm hath spoiled the mighty of his prey ;
His shield of love shall be around and o'er thee,
　　His everlasting strength shall be thy stay ;—
And midst thy dying anguish thou shalt prove
The fulness of His faithfulness and love !

And thus, though pain and sorrow must befall thee,
　　And this poor body turn to dust again,—
Leaning on Him, those pangs shall only call thee
　　With His own ransomed ones in bliss to reign ;
To own the victory His !—and with them praise
His matchless mercy through eternal days.

AGNES.

LINES

ON THE WRECK OF THE AUSTRALIAN STEAM-SHIP,
"LONDON," IN THE BAY OF BISCAY,
January 11th, 1866.

ROUND England's hearths and homes the tempest beats,
　While brighter glows the peace and warmth within ;
And joyously each fireside circle meets,
　Caring but little for the storm's wild din ;
Brightly the young year's life is ushered in,—
　Though farewell words come with its earliest hours ;
And empty chairs show where the loved have been ;
　Some to return with summer's fairest flowers,—
　Some hastening to the land whose own they are,—
　　not ours.

Ah ! little deemed we on that winter's morn,
　How they, the parted ones, were faring then ;
Oh ! could no message on the winds be borne,
　To tell us how that band of noble men,
Wrestling with anguish,—far beyond our ken,
　Hopeless and helpless,—watched each cruel wave,
Knowing o'er them no sun could rise again,
　Yet in their own high courage calm and brave,
　Sinking like heroes, down into a nameless grave.

* Eustace Harwood sailed to and from Australia in this ill-
fated vessel, a few months before his death.

All that the strong man's strength can do or dare,
   Is done to save them,—but is done in vain ;
A stronger arm, a mightier strength is there,
   To guide the tossings of the ruthless main ;
Though woman's tears fall like the falling rain,
   And manhood's prayers ascend in agony,—
No answer comes to bid the waves refrain,
   Or the fierce winds to cease their mastery,—
   The fiat has gone forth ;—those hapless ones must die.

And worth and loveliness,—for *that* was there,—
   The sunlight of so many homes, is fled ;
And who may paint the frenzy of despair,
   With which the crushed and stricken mourners read
Of those last awful hours,—whose deep dread
   Each sorrowing heart in England makes its own :—
Yes ; England mourns her brave and honoured dead,
   Ill can she spare what those wild waves have won,—
   And, weeping, scarce can say, "Father, Thy will be
      done !"

But—Peace be still !—shall we not trust and pray—
   Though that voice came not o'er the surging wave,—
A pitying Saviour was not far away,
   But with them there to succour·and to save,
From the dread triumph of the hungry grave,—
   The yawning chasm,—dark, and deep, and vast,—
In the last conflict they shall ever have,
   He more than conquers,—and, their terrors past,
   Those who have slept in Him, shall wake with joy at
      last !

                                        EVA.

www.ingramcontent.com/pod-product-compliance
Lightning Source LLC
Chambersburg PA
CBHW021133020726
47500CB00003B/1050